W9-BRT-127

THE CHERRY VALLEY MIDDLE SCHOOL NEWS

DEAR KNOW-IT-ALL!

★ ★ ★

Black and White and Gray All Over

by RACHEL WISE

Simon Spotlight
New York   London   Toronto   Sydney   New Delhi

SIMON SPOTLIGHT
An imprint of Simon & Schuster
Children's Publishing Division
1230 Avenue of the Americas,
New York, New York 10020
Copyright © 2013 by Simon & Schuster,
Inc. All rights reserved, including the
right of reproduction in whole or in
part in any form.
SIMON SPOTLIGHT and colophon are
registered trademarks of
Simon & Schuster, Inc.
Text by Elizabeth Doyle Carey
Designed by Bob Steimle

For information about special discounts
for bulk purchases, please contact
Simon & Schuster Special Sales at
1-866-506-1949 or
business@simonandschuster.com.
Manufactured in the United States of
America 0413 FFG
First Edition 10 9 8 7 6 5 4 3 2 1
ISBN 978-1-4424-7515-1 (pbk)
ISBN 978-1-4424-7517-5 (hc)
ISBN 978-1-4424-7518-2 (eBook)
Library of Congress Control Number
2013932717

Chapter 1

FOREIGN STRANGER STEALS GIRL'S LIFE!

★ ★ ★

I don't want to brag, but I think my dream of becoming a reporter one day is well on its way to really happening. I write a lot of articles for the *Cherry Valley Voice*, my middle school newspaper (okay, not just *I*—I write with my supercrush, Michael Lawrence). But our last few articles especially have gotten a lot of praise. Kids stop me in the hall and say things like *I really liked what you wrote about Pay to Play*, or *Way to go on your coverage of the cheating scandal!* It's totally cool and it feels great!

I also get lots of anonymous compliments because I write the advice column called Dear Know-It-All for the paper. No one at school, and I mean *no one*—not even my best friend, Hailey Jones—knows that I am the Know-It-All this year, but I do overhear kids saying really nice things about the Know-It-All responses (*my* responses!) in the paper. All this, plus Mr. Trigg, the faculty advisor for the *Voice*, has taken to automatically giving me and Michael the plum assignments. He calls us the Dream Team, his "star reporters." I love it! Of course, I'd love anything officially linking me with Michael, Mr. Cutie himself.

Sadly, my nearest and dearest just don't get it. Like yesterday I was tutoring Hailey for her grammar exam (she's dyslexic and I always help her with her studying for tests), and I said something flat out, just a fact, and she got annoyed with me. All I said was, "You're lucky your best friend happens to be the best writer in the school." I'm not making it up. It's a fact. But Hailey told me I need to get over myself. I mean, maybe Michael Lawrence is as good a writer as I am, but it's not like he's going to tutor Hailey, right? I was just making conversation, stating the obvious. I don't know why she got so upset about it.

Then at dinner I was telling my mom and my older sister, Allie, about a new writing camp I'd like to attend this summer and how I have to be nominated by a teacher at school in order to apply. I said it's a total no-brainer because Mr. Trigg will do it for me. After all, besides Michael, there's really no one on the newspaper staff who's as good as I am. It's just a fact. But Allie was all snide and said, "Oh, sorry! I forgot about all those Pulitzer Prizes you've won," and my mom (*my very own mom!*) told me not to get a big head. Whatever, people. I am all about facts, and this is just a fact: I'm a great reporter.

Today we have our staff meeting for the next issue, when Mr. Trigg will dole out the assignments for our new articles, and I can't wait. I know I'll get to work with Michael again (hello, quality time with my crushie!), and I know I'll get a juicy, hard-hitting article to report, and I know Mr. Trigg will sing my praises in public like he always does.

I got to the newsroom a little early in order to get a good seat and save a spot for Michael, who always dashes in at the last minute. I snagged the little sofa just inside the door—the best spot— and I spread out my stuff to keep people away from Michael's half of the sofa. Then I pulled out my latest fresh notebook and began making a list of things I needed to do after school today, including stop by the Dear Know-It-All mailbox to collect any new letters and check my bank balance to see if I can afford to buy two new long skirts—kind of my new trademark look—since Allie pointed out that mine are all trashed at the bottom hems. I hate to shop and find it totally boring, plus it kills me to spend money on clothes, but Allie insists on it when the things I own get too dingy.

The newsroom filled up, and sure enough, just as Mr. Trigg came out of his office and strode to the front of the room, Michael popped in the door. He looked at me on the sofa and gestured to the empty spot (as if it wasn't him I was saving it for!). I nodded and quickly cleared my things, and he settled in right next to me, totally cozy. I had to take a moment to think, *This is one of the happiest days of my life.*

I smiled and sighed and turned my attention to Mr. Trigg, who is British and charming and very witty.

"Good morning, gang! Glad to see you all!

Righty-ho, we have lots to discuss today. . . ." He rifled through a pile of papers in his hand and found the one he was looking for. "Aha! Yes! Hmm. Here!" He looked up and scanned the room. Despite Mr. Trigg's kind of careless appearance—his tall, lanky frame stooped as usual, his suit wrinkled and bagging, and his trademark scarf hanging limply around his neck—he is an exacting journalist and an enthusiastic one. He was as excited today as he always is when starting a new issue, and his excitement was contagious.

"I've got an interesting clipping here on year-round school, something I think we should explore. . . ."

There were groans all around the room, but Mr. Trigg shushed everyone with a smile. "It's getting quite popular round the world these days. Hmm. Let's see what this article says. Students receive the same number of vacation days as always. Breaks are more frequent but shorter. . . . Shorter breaks increase knowledge retention. . . . You know, students do tend to forget quite a lot over the summer," he said conversationally. "In addition . . . blah, blah, blah . . . The school buildings don't stand empty. . . . Easier for working parents . . . and so forth. Quite interesting, I daresay. Now, who should it go to . . . ?" He looked up and surveyed the room, and his eyes stopped on me and Michael. I'd known we were going to get it from the moment he started telling us about it. It just felt like a me and Michael article—big, juicy, timely, lots of research. . . .

But suddenly the door to the newsroom opened and everyone looked up.

"Oh, hello! Pardon me, but is this the newspaper meeting?"

In the doorway was a very pretty girl my age. She had black, wavy hair, a pale, creamy complexion, and bright blue eyes, and she spoke with an English accent, to boot! She was smiling and didn't seem at all nervous to be interrupting.

Mr. Trigg was very welcoming. "Well, hello! This *is* the newspaper meeting. Won't you join us, Ms. . . . ?"

"Bigley! Kate Bigley. I was wondering if you

might need any more writers. I've just arrived, transferred in from—"

"Manchester, England, right?" Mr. Trigg interrupted, pointing his finger at her as a huge smile lit up his face.

Kate Bigley laughed and blushed prettily. "Why, yes! And you . . . Liverpool, right?"

Mr. Trigg guffawed and slapped his leg. "Yes, indeed. Well done! Wonderful to have someone from the mother country in our midst! And we've always got room for more reporters."

Kate Bigley said, "That's awfully kind, Mr. . . . ?"

"Trigg. Mr. Trigg. Welcome aboard. Now, we were just discussing an article we'd like to do on year-round schooling. . . ."

"Oh, we have that back home. It was all over the papers when they started. Quite the controversy at first, but everything seems settled now in the schools where they've got it. My friends are all a bit worried it's coming for everyone!" Kate Bigley perched on the arm of the sofa where Michael and I were sitting, and she crossed her legs, settling in. All eyes were on her, but she didn't seem to mind one bit. I don't know why this immediately annoyed me, but it did. As did her sitting right next to Michael without even asking if it was okay. This Kate Bigley was pretty forward.

Mr. Trigg's eyes sparkled. "Well, since you have more experience with the topic than the rest of us, why don't you and Mr. Lawrence, who is seated right next to you, take this on for our next issue? He's got lots of experience and can show you the ropes. You're in very good hands, Ms. Bigley."

Michael nodded up at her, and she smiled back, nodding too.

"Wonderful," she said.

Wonderful? How about *Horrible?!* I wanted to throw up. I felt a hot blush starting, a mix of both anger and mortification. How could Mr. Trigg just cut me out like that? He knew that was my article! How could this girl sandbag him in just minutes, stealing my crush and my assignment in one fell swoop?

All three of them were smiling in the after-

math of their little lovefest, and I was seeth-
ing. I looked around the room to see if other
people noticed the injustice of what had just
happened, but everyone had already turned
their attention back to Mr. Trigg as he started
to hand out the other assignments. He got to
the end of his list and said, "All righty then!
Some words to inspire you from my favorite
fearless leader, Winston Churchill: 'Once in a
while you will stumble upon the truth but most
of us manage to pick ourselves up and hurry
along as if nothing had happened.' I hope that
you all stumble!"

Still chuckling to himself, Mr. Trigg shuffled
his papers again and headed back to his desk in
his little side office off the newsroom. Everyone
started chatting loudly among themselves about
all the new upcoming articles. Even Kate "Fancy
Accent" Bigley and Michael "Traitor" Lawrence
were chatting away, totally oblivious to the fact
that I, the star reporter of the *Cherry Valley Voice*,
the likely editor in chief some day, had just been
totally snubbed in a staff meeting.

Irate, I stood and stalked across the room to Mr. Trigg's office.

"Mr. Trigg," I said, knocking firmly on the door frame.

"Ms. Martone!" he said in a friendly voice, rocking back in his desk chair.

"Mr. Trigg, you didn't give me a story for this issue," I said, trying to control my emotions.

"I didn't?" He shuffled his notes, confused but not bothered by this news. Finding nothing, he turned back to me. "Well, you have been working awfully hard lately, so perhaps a little break is really a blessing in disguise, isn't it?" he said with a chuckle.

"Um, no," I said. Normally I wouldn't mind taking it easy on an issue here and there, but to have Kate Bigley steal my life and me be left swinging in the breeze? No way!

"Hmm. Let's see. Well, I was going to save this for the next issue, but why don't you do an article on school uniforms?"

I looked at him blankly. "What, for here? But this isn't a private school."

"Yes, I know. But it's an interesting topic that schools bring up every now and then. If everyone wore school uniforms, there would be less competition about clothes, less bullying, less teasing. Plus the clothes you buy for recreational wear would last longer, since you wouldn't be wearing them on a daily basis." Mr. Trigg grinned. "I'm sure you'll do a bang-up job with this fashionable topic! Maybe some field research at the mall? Take a few girlfriends along? It's not something I'd assign to one of our male reporters," he said with a wink. "It's a girl special! Just for you!"

"Um . . ." My head was spinning.

"All righty then?" he prompted, turning back to work at his desk.

"Okay, I guess . . . ," I said. In a fog, I drifted out of Trigger's office and through the newsroom, passing Michael Lawrence and Kate Bigley, who were having quite a good time chatting on the sofa, side by side, discussing what should have been my article! Michael didn't even notice me leaving. This was like a bad dream. Out in the hall, I headed off to earthonomics class, still wondering what had just happened in there and knowing I didn't like it. Not one bit.

Foreign Stranger Steals Girl's Life!

Yes, but not for long, I thought. *Not for long.* I needed to find Hailey Jones, my BFF and partner in all discussions boy-related. We needed to discuss the Kate Bigley situation ASAP!

Chapter 2

DESPITE NICKNAME, LITTLE CHICKADEE BATTLES ON

★ ★ ★

I sleepwalked through my morning classes and then I raced to the cafeteria to find Hailey and download everything that had happened in the meeting. I grabbed a tray and blindly chose my lunch—an egg salad wrap from the "healthy option" table—and scanned the room looking for Hailey's bright blond hair. It didn't take long to find her, but she was sitting with Jenna, her NBF. We'd all met during my ill-fated tryout for the gymnastics team a while back, and those two had really hit it off. I don't mind Hailey having other friends, obviously. It's just that I need her to be totally available to me when it's called for. And this is one of those times!

With a huff of frustration, I set out across the room to join them.

"Hey, Sam!" said Jenna as I plunked my tray down on the table.

"What's up?" said Hailey.

"Hey, Jenna. Hey, Hails," I said, nodding seriously. I sat and unwrapped my sandwich, dying to tell Hailey all my news but not really wanting to unload in front of Jenna. I didn't want everyone to know I'd just been dissed for a story, after all. I figured maybe Jenna would need to go get a drink and then I could quickly dish to Hailey. Meanwhile, I needed my strength, so food was in order.

I listened distractedly as the two of them chatted about this new watercolor painting class they're going to take at the Y starting after school today. It was Jenna's idea, and I was a little annoyed by the two of them going off to do it together without me, but I couldn't exactly tell Hailey not to do it. Could I? Hmm. Distracted, I took a look around the cafeteria, only to realize that Michael Lawrence and Kate Bigley were sitting two tables away.

I basically choked on my egg salad when I saw them, Kate laughing at Michael's jokes and Michael speaking earnestly and using his hands to gesture like he does when he's making an important point.

"Are you okay?" Hailey asked, interrupting her conversation with Jenna.

"I'm . . . fine," I said crankily.

"Um, no you're not!" said Hailey, wide-eyed at my tone. "What's the problem?"

I smoldered for a second, debating letting Jenna know my troubles. But I couldn't hold it in anymore. "*That* is my problem!" I said, gesturing with my chin toward Kate and Michael.

Hailey and Jenna turned and looked and then turned back to me, Hailey's eyes as wide as saucers. "*Who* is *that*?" she asked dramatically.

I sighed. Suddenly I felt overwhelmed with exhaustion. I was not dying to get into the whole story. But what could I do?

"That is Kate Bigley, the new star reporter for the *Cherry Valley Voice*," I said in a monotone.

"What?!" cried Hailey, appropriately shocked.

"Since when? Where did she come from?"

"Manchester, England, apparently," I said.

Hailey whipped her head around to take another look. "She's foreign?"

I rolled my eyes. "Barely. I mean, England isn't exactly Tunisia or Jakarta or something. She speaks English, obviously."

"Ooh! Does she have one of those great accents, like Kate Winslet?" asked Jenna in excitement. Right then I hated Jenna.

"Yes, of course," I muttered.

"Wow," said Jenna admiringly.

"It's not like you have to do anything to get one!" I burst out. "You just have to be born there!"

Jenna looked at me warily, but Hailey laughed. "Look, maybe she's cute and she sounds cool, but no one's as good a writer as you, Sammy. You've got that on her."

I rolled my eyes, sure that Hailey was poking fun at me for my comment yesterday.

"For real," said Hailey, meeting my eyes and giving me a serious look. She tipped back in her chair and nodded solemnly, her arms crossed.

"Thanks." I sighed. "But I don't have that on her either. She just stole my assignment for the next issue of the *Voice*." I rested my chin on my hand. My appetite for egg salad had vanished, and the wrap lay discarded half-eaten on my tray.

"What?!" said Hailey. Her chair came back down to earth with a crash.

I nodded. "Trigger was about to assign me and Michael the lead article for the next issue, and in barges the Queen of England and he hands it to her on a silver platter! He didn't even ask for her credentials!"

"Major," said Hailey, shaking her head. I was happy to see that she took this as seriously as I did. "So now what?" she asked.

I shrugged. "I have no idea," I said.

Hailey reached over and patted my hand. "Well, you've still got me," she said.

Jenna nodded. "And me, too."

Humph.

At the end of the day, I swung by the *Voice* office to pick up any Know-It-All letters that might have arrived. If Kate was going to steal my news articles, well, at least she couldn't steal Dear Know-It-All from me. I decided I'd make my Know-It-All column for this issue the best I'd ever done. I might even take up a whole page!

When I got to the office, there was no one there, thank goodness. I quickly locked the door and whipped the three letters from the drop box into my bag; then I unlocked the door and caught my breath. It's always stressful retrieving the letters. If I got caught, my cover would be blown and Mr. Trigg would have to get a new Know-It-All. Being anonymous is what it's all about.

Squaring my shoulders, I opened the door and ran smack into Michael Lawrence.

"Ouch!" he said, rubbing his leg where my messenger bag had whacked him.

"I'm so sorry!" I cried. I always seem to be doing something klutzy when I'm around Michael Lawrence. It's beyond embarrassing.

"In a rush?" he asked.

I hesitated. If I said yes, I wouldn't be able to stay and chat with him. But I was still annoyed with him, so I didn't really *want* to stay and chat with him. I just wanted him to go away.

"Kind of," I said.

"Okay. Bye." He opened the door to the news office.

"Wait!" I said. That had happened all too quickly. He turned back. "Um, how's it going with Kate?"

Michael raised his eyebrows. "Pretty good," he said. "It's hard to tell yet."

"Okay," I said. "Can she write?"

He folded his arms and leaned against the doorjamb. "I don't know. She said she had her own column at the paper back home, so that's pretty impressive. We'll see. It is nice to have someone with a fresh new take on things around here. You know, like an outsider."

Oh. Fresh? New?

I felt like Michael had just punched me in the stomach. I had to get out of there before I cried (and I am not a crier).

"Well, good luck!" I said, all fake cheery, turning to go. "I'm sure it will turn out great!"

"Okay . . . ," he said.

I think Michael was confused by my sudden departure, but with tears pricking at my eyes, I could hardly stay. It was bad enough that they were on the article together and she was this great star reporter, but she had something I'd never have: newness. Michael and I have been in the same class since kindergarten and he might just be sick of me. But there is nothing I can do to change that except move away for ten years and come back with an accent!

I speed-walked out of school and rode my bike home very quickly.

After I stowed my bike in the garage, I climbed the stairs to the first floor and passed Allie in the kitchen.

She said in a teasing voice, "How's the star reporter today?"

I told her to shut up and I kept walking.

"*Wow,*" she said, shaking her head.

Whatever. I knew my mom would make me

apologize to her later, but it felt good to take out my anger on Allie for even a minute.

Upstairs, I flung my bag to the floor, shut my door firmly, and flattened myself facedown on the bed. I felt like everything I'd been working toward had come crashing down. I wasn't a star reporter: I was just a staff writer who was easily replaced by an untested newbie. And I wasn't Michael Lawrence's right hand, edging toward something more: I was just a replaceable writing partner who was stale and overly familiar, not fresh or new like some other people.

The tears of self-pity started to flow.

I wiped myself out with crying—I guess I'm not in good crying shape, because I do it so rarely—and I wound up closing my eyes for just a few minutes. But suddenly it was dark outside and my mom was coming in and waking me up for dinner.

"Sweetheart, time to wake up. I let you sleep for a little while. . . ." She was rubbing my back and speaking in a soothing tone. The light from the hall spilled into my room and made me wince. I was uncomfortable, too, since I'd fallen asleep with my notebook under me at a weird angle.

"Hi," I croaked, turning over. "Can't I just go to bed for the night?"

"No, you need something in your stomach, and I'm sure you must have homework."

I moaned. "I'm tired."

"Maybe you slept too long. What's the matter? Allie said you were cranky when you got home." She sat down on the side of my bed, settling in for a chat.

Ugh. I just wanted to go back to sleep and now this.

"Is it something to do with your classes?" she asked.

I shook my head and stretched.

"Your friends?"

Again, no.

"Is it the paper?"

I was actually surprised she hadn't guessed that first, since I've had a lot of drama this year with the paper. I sighed and nodded.

"What's up, buttercup?" she asked, smoothing my hair back from my face.

I did not want to start crying again, and it was hard to think of how to phrase it so that I wouldn't. I took a deep breath.

"Well . . . there's this new girl at school . . . ," I said, and I started crying.

"Okay, shh. It's okay. You don't have to tell me right now. Why don't you come have something to eat and then you'll feel better?" she said.

I nodded and climbed off my bed.

"Go wash your face and then come down for dinner. It's lentil soup with those crispy broiled bread slices you like, with the olive oil and salt. And some prosciutto."

"Yum!" Suddenly I realized I was starving. I had barely eaten lunch, and anyway, the crying had made me hungry too. ***Relief Worker Saves Weary Girl.***

"Oh, and . . . you still need to apologize to Allie for telling her to shut up."

Snap!

Downstairs, I slid into my seat at the table, apologizing very briefly to Allie. She had obviously been warned not to hassle me, so she accepted, and I ate my dinner in silence, interrupting only to ask for seconds.

Afterward, I did feel much better. I sighed contentedly as my mom passed around a plate of tiny sea-salted, chocolate-covered caramels for dessert, one of my favorites that I know Mom keeps for when I've had a tough day. Maybe it was the chocolate, but after the food was finished, I felt all warm and fuzzy about my family and I decided to tell them what had happened. I didn't even mind telling Allie.

I explained about the British invasion of Kate Bigley, and how Mr. Trigg had given her my article and my writing partner in one fell swoop, while assigning me a girly article on fashion.

"Bummer," said Allie, shaking her head.

My mom was thinking, her hands nested under her chin, a faraway look in her eye.

"Mom?" I asked.

"Oh, I was just thinking about a boss I had back at the big accounting firm where I started out. He'd give the female accountants the easy jobs, or the jobs relating to women's issues or products, while the men got really meaty and exciting assignments and big jobs, like the government projects or software companies. But then he'd have the female accountants meet the clients, walk them to the conference room, and offer them coffee. He said it was just traditional and hospitable, but really an assistant should have done it. It made the clients think less of the women when we took that role from the beginning."

"So what did you do?"

"A bunch of us tried to fight it, but the CEO at the time loved him and we all wound up quitting instead, while he stayed."

"That's terrible!" cried Allie.

"Yes, but we had the last laugh. The next CEO was a woman, and she transferred him to our office in Madrid, Spain, during her first month there! No one has heard from him since!" She laughed.

"I guess she figured *him* out pretty quickly," I said.

"You betcha! *And* she gave me my first

freelance jobs too. What a great lady, a great leader," mused my mom.

"So what do you think about me?" I asked.

"Well, for one thing, I think you need to make the best of the uniform article. Approach it as a hard-hitting news article, not a fashion story. Do lots of research and interviews. And make sure to look at it from a gender-based perspective, to see if there is bias there."

She was onto something. I could tell because my fingers were itching for my notebook to start making a list.

"Okay!" I said excitedly.

"Just really make the most of the assignment. Make it as big as you can. See what happens then," she said.

I was fired up now; ideas were coming every second. "Do you mind if I run up and get my notebook?" I asked.

"It's okay. Go ahead. We'll clean up," said Allie generously.

I looked to make sure she wasn't joking, but she was serious. "Go ahead. I've almost finished my homework anyway," she repeated.

"Thanks!" I said, and I scrambled upstairs to get started before she could change her mind.

Later, when my mom came into my room to say good night, she whispered, "Don't forget that knowing the ropes and having a good, tried and tested reputation are equally as desirable as being new and fresh. They're just different sides of the same coin, okay?"

I nodded, sleepy again.

"Also, make the most of Dear Know-It-All. That's something you've got that no one else has, and you're excellent at it," she said. Besides Mr. Trigg (and possibly Michael Lawrence), my mom was the only person on earth who knew I wrote the column.

"Thanks, Mom. I love you," I said.

"Love you too, little chickadee," she said, and she kissed me good night.

Despite Nickname, Little Chickadee Battles On.

Chapter 3

JOURNALIST GETS REPRIEVE FOR ONE MORE DAY!

★ ★ ★

The next morning, as I organized my bag for school, I realized I hadn't looked at the Know-It-All letters the previous night. I had to take them out and leave them home because they made me nervous in my bag. What if Hailey needed to borrow a pen and went rummaging around in there?

I closed my door and got the envelope out from behind my desk, where I stash all Know-It-All correspondence, but I couldn't just shove them in without even a quick peek. I am a reporter, after all, and naturally curious!

The first one was on lime-green stationery, handwritten, and very girly. It said:

Dear Know-It-All,

My dog misses me so much when I go to school. She chases the school bus when I leave, and my mom says she whines by the door all day until I come home. Why can't we have a Bring Your Pets to School day? I think it would help my dog if she could see where I go when I'm not with her.

From,

Madison Jones

Okay, first of all, Madison, this is supposed to be anonymous, my friend. Second of all, how do we know Rover won't bite some kid, if she's as attached to you as you say?

I sighed and dropped that one into the big envelope. That one was definitely *not* going to make me shine as an advice columnist, and in this issue I needed to shine!

The next one was in scratchy boy handwriting on loose-leaf paper. It said:

Dear Know-It-ALL,

My clothes stink. I hate everything my mom buys. It's superpreppy and I want to dress gangsta, but she says that's inappropriate for school. The dress code says we're allowed to wear sweats and stuff, so why shouldn't she let me? Maybe if you print this I can show her your response (if you're on my side).

Thanks,

A dude

Hmm. That was very tempting. But I don't want to pigeonhole myself as a fashion writer. I jammed it in the file.

The final one was dumb. It was on a postcard from Las Vegas and it said:

Dear Know-It-All,

Why can't we have more vacation?

From,

Vegas Girl

Whatever, Vegas Girl. If the year-round-school people get their way, you're really going to be sorry.

I sighed and stuffed the letters all into the big secret envelope, wishing I could give the Vegas postcard to Michael for his article research, but that would blow my cover. Anyway, why would I want to help him and Miss Big(ley)?

After classes ended, I popped into the news office to see if I could check for more Know-It-All submissions, but I was out of luck—or maybe in luck: Michael Lawrence was there sitting at a computer, so I was unable to check my mailbox.

My heart leaped when I saw him, but he looked weary and not that happy. He was rubbing his eyes and slumping in his chair.

I decided to keep it fresh and new.

"Hey, Michael," I said. (I usually call him Mikey, or just Lawrence.)

He looked up. "Yo, Pasty."

So much for fresh and new. Pasty is the nickname he gave me when I was caught eating paste in kindergarten. I grimaced but pressed on.

"What are you up to?"

He sighed. "Just trying to make sense of Kate's notes for the article. We interviewed Mr. Pfeiffer this morning to see what his thoughts are, as principal, on year-round school."

"Are you transcribing her notes?" I asked, peering over his shoulder. I couldn't keep my eyebrows from shooting up. Michael doesn't take notes because his memory is incredible. I usually *do* take notes, and he used to mock me for always writing everything down. But then one time it actually came out to be a good thing that I did, since we ended up needing the notes for reference. Still, this was very out of character for him.

Michael nodded wearily. "But I can't make heads or tails of them. It's all scribble scrabble."

"Why isn't she doing it? Wouldn't that be easier?" I felt a little annoyed seeing Kate's notes in front of him.

He nodded again. "Yes. It would. But she's 'frightfully busy' right now getting acclimated, so I guess I volunteered, though I don't remember volunteering."

I had to laugh, he looked so sad. "It's not the end of the world, Mikey," I said. "Just bounce them back to her. Tell her you can't read her British handwriting."

He sighed again. "You think?"

"Yes, I do. Do it!"

"Why are women always so bossy?" he said, shaking his head. But he stood up and shoved the notes in his backpack.

"I object to that gross generalization!" I said, putting my hands on my hips.

Michael laughed and put his palms up in the "I surrender" pose. "You're right! Let me correct myself. Why are *you* always so bossy?"

"Wow, not much better," I said, and he laughed. I had to smile. It was feeling like old times again.

"Are you heading out?" he asked, and my stomach filled with butterflies. Maybe we'd get to spend some quality time together! That would certainly help take his mind off Ms. Bigley.

"Yes, actually I'm . . ." I was going to invite him to go walk around outside school with me to do some research for my article. Then maybe that would lead to other things, and we'd go get a Gatorade together or something. But the door swung open and it was Kate Bigley herself.

"What's up, Mickey L.?" she said cheerily in that accent of hers.

Mickey L.?

"Hey," said Michael sheepishly. "I'd actually just given up on your notes and was leaving."

"Given up? Where I come from, we never give up! Just think of what Mr. Trigg's chum Winston Churchill said. 'Never, ever, ever, ever, ever, ever, ever give up. Never give up. Never give up. Never give up.'" Kate laughed.

No wonder she and Trigg hit it off, I thought grimly.

"Right," said Michael.

"So let's have a go at it, shall we?" she said, settling her things on the sofa.

Michael looked at me, then back at Kate. "I guess so," he said. "Sorry, Sam."

He never calls me Sam. This was not good. Not good at all. I cast around for a way to salvage our outing, but my brain wasn't working fast enough.

"Okay. Bye," I said. But I purposely didn't say "good luck," because I didn't wish them any. I hated Michael right then. I closed the door after myself and slouched toward my locker. As I drew near, I spied Hailey up ahead, loading her things into her backpack. Thank goodness! I nearly ran the final thirty yards.

"Hails!" I called. "Want to go interview subjects with me?"

"Hey! No, sorry. I can't! Jenna and I have to go do our watercolor homework. We're supposed to go out in nature and paint something alive. Cool, right?"

"Can't you do that any old time?" I asked, sighing loudly. I knew I was being spoiled and pouty, but I needed her right then.

"No, because we want to go together, and it's the only day we both have free before the next class. By the way, the class was great. Thanks for asking." She shut her locker and lifted her backpack onto one shoulder.

"Sorry," I said, wincing at my forgetfulness. "How was it?"

"Great! And guess what? I'm really good at it!"

I couldn't help but be annoyed at Hailey for bragging after she'd harshed on me for it only days earlier. "Oh, who's bragging now?" I asked, but I used a joking voice.

Hailey grinned, taking it good-naturedly. "I know. I know. But the thing is, it feels so *good* to be good at something. I mean, besides soccer, but I've been playing that since I was a baby practically. This is something new. With school being so hard for me, I'm just not used to having something come so easily. I guess watercolors for me are like writing for you. We're just naturally very talented at it!"

I felt a little insulted. "Writing doesn't come that easily for me, though. I mean, I do work really hard at it."

"I know you do, but you also enjoy that part of it. I work hard at soccer, too. And I work hard at painting, but it comes easily at the same time."

I knew I had to be happy for Hailey. I rose above my irritation for a minute and did the right thing. "That's great," I said. "Make a picture for me next. Something good, okay?"

Hailey grinned and hugged me sideways. "Thanks! I will. You'll love it. I promise."

Jenna came up and we said hi, and then with a pang, I watched them walk off together. Jenna and Hailey. Michael and Miss Big. I pulled my clipboard out of my locker, snagged a pen from my messenger bag, and went to interview kids outside school about the idea of uniforms.

It's funny, but even though I'm naturally kind of shy, when I'm reporting for an article, I'm not shy at all. It's like I have the *Cherry Valley Voice* to hide behind, so it's not really me who's doing the interviewing and stuff; I'm just the mouthpiece for the paper. It gives me courage.

Like, normally I wouldn't approach kids I don't know outside school, but today it was no problem. I pinned on this big press badge that Mr. Trigg had given me at one point, and I was good to go. Then, with my pen in hand, I stopped kids and asked them questions I'd come up with during math class when I was supposed to be listening to the teacher. They were:

- How would you feel if our school adopted uniforms?
- If you are for it or wouldn't mind, what kind would you like to have?
- If you are against it, why?
- Do you have any other comments you'd like to add?

Kids were pretty willing to speak out on the subject, and the interesting thing was that most of the girls were for it and the boys were against it. I asked one really popular girl, Della Pollen, and she thought it would be a good idea because then she wouldn't have to worry about what to wear in the mornings. Another girl, Trina Jones, said if we had uniforms then she could save money or spend it on other things instead of trying to buy trendy clothes for school. Two girls who were dressed really cool said they'd hate uniforms, and I could easily see why, though one pointed out that if we had a uniform she'd never be late again, since it wouldn't take so long to get dressed in the morning! This was turning out to be a surprising assignment.

A quiet girl named Pam from my language arts class said it would be a good equalizer, so the nerdy and the cool and the kids who spent a lot and those who couldn't would all look the same and we could judge people on themselves rather than their clothes. I thought that was a really good answer, but she didn't want her quote to be used for attribution, which in reporter-speak means I could use it but not say who said it.

The girls who were "for" uniforms all thought a plain skirt maybe in gray flannel material plus a solid-colored polo shirt or blouse on top would be just right, with some footwear restrictions but not requirements.

But the boys I interviewed were *not* into the idea of uniforms at all. Tommy Sheehan felt that the boy uniform options were dorky—ties, flannel pants, blazers, and button-down shirts were not appealing at all. Santi Diaz said that boy uniforms looked uncomfortable and like they'd restrict his movements. Kevin Kurtz didn't like the idea of being told what to wear because it was unconstitutional and threatened his freedom of expression.

I put a star next to his answer; I thought that was a really good point.

Other people I talked with told little anecdotes about their cousins who had to wear uniforms or friends they knew at private or parochial schools who had them. Some kids swore the uniform wearers hated it; others said for sure they loved it. It seemed kind of evenly split. I made a mental note to have Hailey help me do a poll on Buddybook to get a broader idea of what people thought. (I hate Buddybook because I think it's a time suck, but it's good for stuff like this. That's why I don't have my own account anymore. I just use Hailey's or Michael's if I need it for research.) In all, I'd interviewed about fifteen kids, pretty evenly split between boys and girls, and I had some good points. I sat on the wall by the bike rack and cleaned up my messy notes so I could make sure I got the quotations right. A bunch of kids were still milling around, getting their bikes out of the rack. I was waiting to see if maybe some more kids would come by when I saw Michael and Kate walk out together. I felt my stomach drop when I saw them, but they couldn't really see me, since I was behind them and hidden by the bustle of the bike rack.

Please don't let them leave together, I hoped silently. *Please!*

As I watched them intently, two girls unlocking their bikes in front of me saw them too.

One of them said, "Michael Lawrence has a new girlfriend. Bummer."

The other said, "New? Who was the old one?"

"Oh, I think that girl from the paper he's always with."

I held my breath and turned my face away so they wouldn't see me. My cheeks were flushed deep red, and I strained to catch every word they said.

The second girl said, "No, she's not his girlfriend. I know they write together a lot. Maybe she's, like, his best friend."

"Sure looked like a girlfriend to me!"

"Well, I don't know about her, but I think *this* one is for sure," said the second girl.

"Why?"

"Just . . . I've seen them together a few different times this week."

"Well, were they acting all lovey-dovey or what?" said the first girl, exasperated.

"No."

"You think every time you see a boy and a girl together that they're dating. But boys and girls can be just friends, you know," huffed the first girl.

And they hopped on their bikes and left.

I wanted to throw up. I hardly dared turn around because I did not want to see Michael Lawrence, love of my life, stroll off with Kate Bigley. It wasn't that he didn't have the right to. I mean, we'd never dated or anything, and I'd certainly never declared my love to him, which I suddenly regretted.

Inch by inch I turned my head until I could see them. And then I let out a huge sigh of relief. Michael was heading home and Kate Bigley was walking away in the opposite direction. Thank goodness! *Journalist Gets Reprieve for One More Day!* I had to stop my imagination from running wild.

Things were not going my way. I needed some advice, and there was only one place to turn.

Chapter 4

JOURNALIST'S BRAIN EXPLODES FROM CONFUSION

★ ★ ★

Allie and I were eating our pizza at the kitchen table when my mom swept in looking really pretty and smelling like her fancy perfume. She kissed us sideways so she wouldn't get lipstick on us, and she cautioned us to finish our homework and not fool around just because she was going to her book club. And then she was gone and Allie returned to her lecture.

"See, part of the problem is you've gotten lazy. You're used to letting Mr. Trigg do all the work for you, assigning you articles together and whatnot," she was saying. She peeled a piece of pepperoni off her slice and dangled it into her mouth.

"Gross," I said, and she shrugged and ate it.

"Yes, it's all Trigger's fault," I said, fake mad.

"That sexist!" joked Allie.

But I was serious now. "Do you think he is?" I asked.

Allie nodded, chewing her pizza. "I think what he said was," she said, swallowing. "And you should call him on it. I mean, he's not as bad as that old boss of Mom's, but he might get worse. You should nip it in the bud."

"Like, I should go talk to him?" The idea made me nervous. Sure, I've talked to Trigger about tons of stuff before, but accusing him of being sexist seemed pretty heavy.

"Yeah. It doesn't have to be a big deal. Just tell him he insulted you and that you hope in the future he'll be careful to keep his comments and assignments as unbiased and gender neutral as the *Cherry Valley Voice* tries to be."

I had to admire Allie's way with words. It didn't sound confrontational that way. "Very well put, Allie Cat!"

"Not everything has to be made into a federal case, as long as you get your point across."

"True. I want to keep getting articles from him anyway, so he can't be my enemy. Just no more fashion stuff!"

"Right. And lots more coauthorship with Michael." She laughed. "By the way, I don't think uniforms would be the worst thing in the world," Allie added as she sat back down at the table.

"You don't?!" I was surprised, to say the least. Allie is so fashion conscious, I thought she would have come down on the side of freedom of expression in this case.

"No. Sometimes there's too much focus on what to wear or who is wearing what, and with a uniform you could concentrate more on school, without the distraction. Just keep it simple."

"So you're saying people might do better in school if they didn't have to worry about their clothes?"

"Maybe not to that extreme, but there'd definitely be more time in the morning if I didn't have to go make sure my shoes matched my outfit, I had the right accessories, and I was wearing the latest trend. You know, things like that."

"Interesting, especially coming from you!" I said. "I would have thought you'd be anti-uniform."

Allie laughed. "Never presume to know what a girl thinks until you've walked a mile in her stilettos. Remember that!"

"Oh boy," I said, rolling my eyes. "So what should I do about Michael?"

Allie tilted her head and thought. "You said you haven't seen much of him, right?"

I nodded.

"You said he looked frustrated when you saw him in the office because Kate had dumped the work on him?"

"Uh-huh."

"You said they didn't walk off together after school?"

"Yes!" I sighed dramatically.

Allie tapped her chin, thinking. "Okay. Do nothing."

"What?" I was confused.

"Do nothing," Allie repeated.

I was stunned. "I do *nothing* while Miss UK steals the love of my life?"

"That's right!" said Allie, standing again and stretching.

"But why?" I said frantically.

"You just wait and see," said Allie mysteriously. "Trust me. Things are going to go your way." And she left, leaving me sitting at the table stumped. *Journalist's Brain Explodes from Confusion.*

Huh.

The next day I nearly stabbed Hailey with my fork at lunch in the cafeteria.

How's that for a lead sentence? A lead (rhymes with *steed*, not head) is the first line a journalist writes in an article. It's meant to grab the reader's attention and also answer the five W's of journalism: Who, What, When, Where, and Why.

Who: Hailey and I

What: Fork stabbing

When: Lunchtime

Where: The cafeteria

Why: It's complicated. (Okay, the lead didn't answer that, but I will now.)

Here's why: Hailey and I were finally having a fun lunch, just the two of us—no Jenna, no Kristen or Meg or Tricia or any randoms, just a good old-fashioned catch-up between besties. I didn't even mention Michael Lawrence. It was that good. We talked about the school uniform thing, and Hailey said she liked Allie's "keep it simple" concept. She'd be *for* uniforms, but preferred a pants option for girls, of course. We talked about her watercolor class and how nice the teacher is and how most of the other students are adults and one is this really cute college guy who's nice to her and Jenna and shows them how to perfect their techniques. We chatted on and on, and then Kate Bigley walked into the cafeteria. My eyes instinctively searched the room for Michael Lawrence, but to my relief he was sitting with his whole basketball team at a table way off in the corner. You'd have to really know what you were looking for to find him, because he was pretty hidden.

Kate got her lunch and stood with her tray in her hand, looking around for a place to sit.

Hailey spotted her and said, "Hey, there's that girl who stole your life."

We looked at Kate in silence for a second, and then Hailey said quietly, "She's actually pretty nice. She was cracking me up in PE yesterday."

I rolled my eyes. "She isn't that nice; trust me."

"I hate to ask, but do you really think it was her fault that Mr. Trigg assigned her the article?"

I scoffed and shifted uncomfortably in my seat. I guess that wasn't *technically* her fault, but she could have turned him down.

"Oh, great. Now she's looking this way," said Hailey. "The poor thing. She has nowhere to go. I'm waving her over."

And before I could stop her, Hailey was up out of her seat, waving Kate Bigley to our table.

Kate smiled a huge smile of relief and headed our way.

"Hailey!" I hissed. ***Journalist Stabs Former Best Friend with Fork.***

"Samantha Martone, you should be ashamed

of yourself. How would you like to be new in a foreign school in a foreign country?" said Hailey indignantly.

"But she stole my—" I couldn't finish because Kate was upon us.

"Hello! Thank you ever so much! I felt like such a dolt standing there with no friends," Kate chattered as she sat down.

"No problema," said Hailey. "That's American for 'no problem,' by the way," she said graciously.

"Hailey!" I laughed in spite of myself. "That's Spanish, you dope!"

"Oh, whatever. I'm dyslexic," she announced. Hailey always made that announcement up front when she met new people. I think it took the pressure off her a little, and it kept things from getting awkward in case someone said or asked the wrong thing.

"Really? So's my brother," said Kate, taking a bite out of a big turkey sandwich. The girl had an appetite, judging from what was on her tray. My feelings toward her softened a millimeter based on just that. I really can't stand tiny salad eaters. I mean, come on! I know they're hungry! Why won't they just admit it?

The two of them launched into discussing the special boarding school Kate's brother had started attending in the fourth grade and how it had changed his life.

"I really think he was depressed before. He always felt dumb, the poor bloke, even though he was a star on the cricket pitch and the football field. Now he knows he's smart as anything and he just needs to approach things sideways rather than head-on. I've bet him he'll end up at Oxford."

Hailey was fascinated, and I could see she wanted to learn more.

I hadn't said anything yet and it was a little awkward. "So it's pretty funny that you ended up as a writer, with your brother having such a hard time of it," I said.

"I know. We always joke about it. We complement each other. I need him for sports and activity encouragement, and he needs me to proofread his work."

Hailey and I smiled at each other. "That's like us!" said Hailey.

"I love writing," I said, warming to the conversation in spite of myself.

"Oh, me too," agreed Kate, beginning a bowl of fruit salad. "And Mr. Trigg is so nice. I'm not just saying that because he's British, either."

"I know. He's great. But I'm a little annoyed with him right now," I said.

Hailey shot me a warning look, but I wasn't going to bring up Kate's article, obviously. Just the sexist thing.

"Why?" asked Kate.

I winced. "Well . . . he made a pretty sexist comment, and it bothered me," I said. And I filled her in.

"Wow. I can't believe that. You should stand up to him on that," she said. Her eyebrows arched and her cheeks turned pink. "Just on principle. But the truth is"—her voice lowered to a whisper—"girls really do tend to like fashion more than boys do, right?" She giggled.

I smiled a little. "I guess," I said. It made me

think for a minute: Was I madder at Trigger for giving my article to Kate, or for the sexist comment? It was hard to say.

"I'm still jealous you got that article," said Kate.

What?

I swallowed hard. "Why?" I asked, trying to keep the shock out of my voice.

Kate's bright blue eyes sparkled. "My dream is to be an entertainment reporter. I absolutely *love* writing articles about celebrities and lifestyle and, most of all, fashion. Anything to do with clothes is right up my alley. Not that it isn't fun working with Michael," she added.

I'd been growing comfortable with our conversation, and now I felt like I'd been punched. And anyway, what was that supposed to mean? They *were* having fun? Or *weren't* they? Was she saying it just to be nice or bragging? I couldn't tell.

"Oh," I said. "Yes." I searched Kate's face for clues, but she looked neutral.

"I'd love your advice sometime on all this, by the way," said Kate. Her eyes were downcast as she toyed with the brownie on her plate.

"Sure," I said stiffly. Advice on what? Michael? The paper? Was she going to ask for tips on how to get him to ask her out? OMG.

"Well, as much as I find it fascinating to hear you two talk about journalism," said Hailey dryly, "it's time for me to head off to language arts. Have fun in earthonomics, Sam."

Kate laughed. "Where on earth do you get these class titles?"

"Ha! Read Sam's article!" Hailey picked up her tray and took off. "Catch ya later, Martone," she called out over her shoulder.

"Is there an article?" asked Kate.

I tried to relax and forget that Kate might be in love with my crush. Other than that, she was pretty nice and we definitely had some common interests.

"Yes, when they changed it all around in the fall, Trigger had us—Michael and me—write an article about it. It was pretty heated," I admitted, smiling at the memory of all the drama that surrounded not only the curriculum changes but

Michael's and my reporting of it. I wondered now if we'd ever have that opportunity again.

"Aha! One of the famous Martone/Lawrence stories! I can't wait to read it!" said Kate brightly. "I'll look it up in the archive."

We brought our trays to the window and headed out together. I glanced at the table where Michael had been sitting, hoping he'd see his former and current partners walking together and worry what we were saying about him, but I was out of luck. He was gone.

As we walked to class, Kate began to fill me in a tiny bit on how homesick she was, how awkward she'd been feeling as the new girl, and how grateful she was to have stopped by the newspaper office, since it gave her a reason to talk to people. I hadn't thought of it that way before. Certainly I'd seen how it would be scary and lonely to start at a new school, but the newspaper—or any activity, for that matter—did give you a good "in" for finding people you'd have something in common with. But I'd assumed she was a hotshot journalist looking to show off her skills and teach us Americans a little thing or two about how they do it on Fleet Street (that's the journalism capital of London). Little did I know.

I guess what Allie had said was true: You do have to walk a mile in someone's stilettos to know what they're going through. Who knew Allie would be the soul of sensitivity?

We reached my classroom door, and Kate said, "Thanks so much for letting me sit with you girls today. I had a lovely time."

"Yeah, that was fun," I said, surprised but kind of meaning it.

"We should get together again and you can fill me in on the paper and everyone there and how it all runs," she said.

"Okay," I agreed. It might be nice to have a good girlfriend on the paper, I suddenly realized. Someone who loves writing as much as I do, someone who shares my interests, the way Hailey now has Jenna.

"Great. Because I was on track to be editor in chief at my school paper, and now my mom is pushing me to go out for it here." She laughed. "Is your mom pushy?"

But the blood had drained out of my head. "Um. No," I said distractedly. *Editor in chief?* But that was going to be *my* job. I felt sick suddenly and needed to sit down. "Okay, bye," I said.

"Toodles!" said Kate, and she walked off.

Toodles?

Oh dear.

I don't even remember what we learned in earthonomics that day. Only that I bit my nails down to nubs, something I hadn't done in a year. ***Job Security Threatened, Journalist Caves.***

Chapter 5

SPY MAKES THE MOST OF HIDDEN OUTPOST

★ ★ ★

The next day I ran into Michael in the hall at my locker. I don't know why he was down there since his locker is way at the other end of the hall. I was bursting with joy at seeing him but also generally kind of angry at him for being joined with Kate, even if it hadn't been his choice.

"What's up, Pasty?" he asked.

"Not much, Mikey," I said, playing it cool. "Haven't seen much of you lately." He looked away, then looked back at me.

"Yeah," I agreed. *You don't seem that upset, since you have a replacement,* I wanted to yell.

He looked away again. "I guess we only see each other when Trigg sets it up," he added.

My head snapped up and I searched his face, but it was neutral. Was he saying he liked that or didn't? I couldn't tell. "I guess so," I agreed.

There was an awkward pause, and I got the sense I was supposed to be saying something, but I didn't know what. What I wanted to say was, *I know, and that's pathetic, since I love you. Now, let's go to the movies on Friday and forget all this!* But I didn't. I couldn't.

"Well . . ."

"How's your . . ."

We both spoke at the same time, then laughed. "You first," he said.

"Oh, I was just going to ask you how the article's going," I said neutrally, like I was just being polite.

"You know. It's good. It's a lot of work."

"Isn't it always?" I groaned.

He looked at me. "I guess it is. I hadn't really thought of it that way before."

Had I just offended him? I wasn't sure. Oh dear. "Well, I mean . . . it's fun and all. It's just, you know, all the notes and the interviewing and the quotes and the surveys and the research, then the writing. . . ." I was babbling now.

"Yeah. Kate told me about what Trigger said, by the way. The sexist comment. That's bad."

What? Kate had already told him? *When?*

"Right. I know. I'll say something." Now I wanted to just get away. I felt betrayed in all directions. "Um, where are you headed now?" I asked, now desperate to wrap this up. I was sick of the Michael and Kate thing, and I couldn't be late for my next class.

"Oh, I'm heading to earthonomics," he said.

"Okay. Well . . ."

"Yeah. Bye," he said.

We both trudged away in opposite directions, and even though I was annoyed with everyone, the overwhelming feeling I had in parting was sadness and loneliness. And like I'd missed something, but I couldn't quite put my finger on what.

★   ★   ★

At lunch I wanted to avoid everyone. I didn't need Michael's weirdness, Kate's aggressive friendliness, or Hailey's pity party for Kate. They were all annoying. ***Independent Journalist Strikes Out on Her Own.***

I decided to grab a quick sandwich to go, stop by the newsroom and pick up any Know-It-All letters, then head to the library to get organized. I'd lain awake half the night, stressing about Kate Bigley, her article with Michael, and the editor in chief job. When I awoke this morning, I knew that the only thing to do was write a huge Know-It-All column for this issue that would blow everyone away and a school uniforms article so impressive that it would make the front page.

I wolfed down my sandwich on a bench in the hall and then ducked into the newsroom. No one was there, so I locked the door and quickly pulled two letters out of the Know-It-All box. But as I was tucking them into my bag, the door handle rattled. Someone was trying to get in.

Gulping, I silently closed the Know-It-All mailbox and thought quickly. Should I hide and let the people open the office door with a key, or should I open it and fake that it had gotten locked behind me? Not that many people had keys to the office, but a few did, like Mr. Trigg, obviously, and Susannah Johnson, the current editor in chief, and maybe one or two other people. If anyone found me in there with the door locked, they'd think only one thing: that I was Dear Know-It-All. I couldn't let that happen. If I blew my cover now, I'd lose the column and Mr. Trigg would probably give it to Kate!

That was all it took for me to reach my decision. I ducked into Mr. Trigg's office and closed the door most of the way without turning on the light, just in time to hear a key turn in the lock and people entering. I fervently hoped it wasn't Mr. Trigg, because he'd really wonder what I was doing in his office.

But it wasn't Mr. Trigg. It was Kate and Michael!

"Okay, it won't take a minute to find this," said Michael.

"Fine," said Kate. "In the meantime, I want to look up the curriculum article by the famous Michael Lawrence and Sam Martone."

My ears pricked up at hearing my name.

"Oh, yeah. That was a good one," said Michael.

"Weren't they all?" said Kate dryly.

What was that supposed to mean?

I could hear typing and I held perfectly still. I hoped this wouldn't take long!

I looked around Mr. Trigg's office, where I'd been many times before. The walls were covered with British memorabilia: his Winston Churchill quotes, his photos and postcards of scenes from London, his "Keep Calm and Carry On" poster, the Union Jack. I realized at that exact moment how much Mr. Trigg loved his home country. He must be really homesick. He was always so jolly and chipper, but he did speak of England in such reverent tones. No wonder he'd been ecstatic to hear Kate's accent. I'd never really thought of him as a person with feelings, so it was weird, but it made me think again of what Allie had said about walking a mile in someone's stilettos (or in Mr. Trigg's case, his dorky desert boots). Who would ever believe that Allie's advice would become so important? Still, he had made that sexist comment, so I didn't want

to go feeling too sorry for him.

Outside, Kate and Michael began talking again and I strained to listen. ***Spy Makes the Most of Hidden Outpost.***

"This is quite good," Kate was saying admiringly. My ears twitched. Was she talking about my article?

"Yeah, Sam's . . . ," began Michael. But he didn't continue.

Sam's what? I wanted to yell. *Sam's great? Sam's a nerd? Sam's better than you? Sam's over?*

I was dying to peek out and see what he was doing that wouldn't let him finish his sentence. I pictured his head bent, his dark hair falling over his brow, his blue eyes squinched in concentration as he typed quickly with two fingers.

"Who does the writing between you two?" asked Kate.

"Umm . . . we both kind of do," said Michael.

"Isn't that difficult to pull off?" asked Kate.

I leaned against Trigg's wall, fascinated but feeling guilty, sick, and scared for the hiding and eavesdropping.

"No, it just kind of works. I don't know," replied Michael. I could picture him shrugging, his shoulders popping up once, then down.

"Hmm," said Kate. "So who does all the research for a big article like this? How do you divide it up?" she asked.

Michael laughed. "Both of us. It just seems to work out."

"Your school papers are a little more . . . professional than ours were back home," said Kate.

Oh, really? Good to know, I thought.

"How so?" asked Michael.

"Just a lot more interviewing people, research, the polls you take. It's like real journalism."

Michael laughed again. "That's the point, isn't it? Don't you want our newspaper to look as professional as possible?"

"I guess so. Our paper was more about popular culture and everyone having a chance to write," said Kate.

They were quiet, and I silently tried to send them brain waves to wrap it up and leave.

"Okay, that should do it," said Michael. "Ready."

Thank goodness!

"Almost finished," said Kate.

Hurry, hurry! I mentally telegraphed to them. *Get out!*

"Hey, guys!"

"Hi, Jeff!"

Oh no! The photo editor, Jeff Perry, had arrived! I suddenly realized I might be trapped here all day. I closed my eyes and sank down against the wall.

"What's up?" asked Michael.

"Just picking up a contact sheet," said Jeff. "Where's Sam?"

My eyes snapped open and my heart thudded.

"Don't know," said Michael briskly.

"I'm sure she's very busy," said Kate.

What was that supposed to mean?

"So let's meet at eleven thirty to interview the head teacher tomorrow," said Michael.

"Oh bother. I can't go then. I've got a cello lesson. So sorry. Any other times work for you?"

"Okay, how about after school Thursday?"

"Soccer club."

"Hmm," said Michael. "We've got to get this done."

"I don't mind if you do it without me. We can just discuss it afterward," said Kate.

"O-kaaayy . . . ," said Michael.

"Bye, guys! Good luck!" said Jeff.

"We're leaving too," said Michael firmly.

There was some rustling; then the lights went off and the door shut. I waited an extra three seconds to be sure they were gone, and then I ducked out of Trigg's office. And it was a lucky thing, too, because literally two seconds later the newsroom door opened and in walked Trigger himself.

He clicked on the lights and blinked at me.

"Ms. Martone! What a pleasant surprise! What are you up to?"

"Uh . . . hi, Mr. Trigg." I gulped nervously but tried not to show it. "I was just hiding some letters in my bag." I patted my messenger bag.

"Good! Hope you got some juicy ones," he said, crossing the room to his office door.

"Me too," I said weakly.

"How's the uniform piece coming along?" he called over his shoulder. "Any fun field trips to the mall with your girlfriends?"

Suddenly my blood boiled.

"Mr. Trigg, can we talk for a minute?" I followed him back to his office door as he snapped on his desk lamp. *Keep calm and carry on,* I told myself.

"Certainly. What's up?"

"Well . . . I . . . I . . ." I stammered, wishing I'd given myself a moment to think of what I needed to say to him.

He looked at me expectantly.

"I think it's a little, uh, sexist of you to keep bringing up the mall and shopping with girlfriends, and everything, in light of this being a serious journalistic article." I bit my lip, knowing my face had turned red and hating myself for it. "And me being a serious journalist," I added.

Mr. Trigg's expression turned to confusion and then surprise.

"Why, Ms. Martone! I'm so very sorry! I hadn't

seen it that way at all!" He looked off in the distance and seemed to be thinking.

"Well, I did," I said quietly.

"I suppose you're right, and I do apologize," said Mr. Trigg quietly. "That was awfully insensitive of me. But quite honestly, I hadn't been thinking of it that way. I'd more been thinking that you work so hard, you track down every lead, you interview every possible subject, you dot every *i* and cross every *t*, and sometimes I think you need to have a little more fun in your life. That was what I'd hoped you'd do with this article."

"Oh," I said. Now I was the surprised one. "I thought it kind of belittled me and my skills."

"My goodness, no! You're the best reporter we have! I rely on you and am constantly adjusting my expectations upward as you continue to surprise me with what you deliver."

"Well, it's me and Michael together, mostly," I said modestly, but inside I was jumping for joy.

"Ms. Martone, I will henceforth maintain gender neutrality at all costs. I am ashamed to see that I have not done so in the past. I hope that you will forgive me and continue to deliver the wonderful work we've all grown accustomed to around here."

"Thank you, Mr. Trigg. I appreciate that."

"How is the uniform piece going, by the way?" he asked.

"Well . . ." I looked up at the wall. "Let's just say I'm keeping calm and carrying on," I said with a smile.

"I would expect nothing less, Ms. Martone," Mr. Trigg said with a smile. "Nothing less, indeed."

Chapter 6

TABLOID SHOWDOWN PITS JOURNALISTS AGAINST EACH OTHER IN RACE TO THE TOP!

★ ★ ★

My two new Dear Know-It-All letters weren't much juicier than the last three. I assumed the first one was from a guy because it was on notebook paper and had scratchy handwriting, but I realized it was sexist of me to assume that guys have bad stationery and bad handwriting while girls have good stationery and good handwriting. So I don't know who it was from! But here's what it said:

Dear Know-It-ALL,

Why do there have to be so many tests? Can't we have fewer?

FROM,

ALWays Studying

Yes, Always, I agree, there are lots of tests. But I don't want to waste this important column making a case against the one thing students have been complaining about since the dawn of time. Maybe on a slow news day, but not now, when so much is riding on this being a great column. ***Tabloid Showdown Pits Journalists Against Each Other in Race to the Top!***

The next letter was eerily applicable to my own life, but not that juicy either. It said:

Dear Know-It-All,

I miss my friend. We used to spend a lot of time together, but now we're both busy with other things and other people and I don't see her very often. I'm not sure what to say or do. Any advice?

Feeling Left Out and Lonely

It made me think of Michael *and* Hailey, as well as Jenna and Kate, of course. It was difficult to know what to say to a friend in this situation that didn't make you sound pouty and jealous or like a loser. An answer to this letter would involve comforting the writer and saying that I'm sure your friend feels the same way and you should plan a fun activity for you both to do, to catch up. But would I take that advice myself? In the case of Hailey, maybe, though I'd hate it if she asked if Jenna could be included. Then I'd be mad.

In the case of Michael, I think I'd be too nervous to actually suggest a plan. It would be like asking him on a date, even though we are only friends and I do miss him. Ugh.

I guess the answer is that it would depend on what kind of friends you are and what you're used to doing with that friend. Not exactly a juicy answer. Ho-hum.

Bored and stumped, I left my desk, hid the letters, and went to talk to my mom, who was working in the den.

"Hi, honey!" My mom is always happy to see

me, I must say. It's a good feeling.

"How's the project going?" She's working on a freelance audit of a local car wash that's being sold. Bor-ing, if you ask me, but she thinks it's fascinating.

"Great! I had no idea how much goes into running a car wash!" she said with a smile. "What's up with you?"

"I am just feeling like I have no friends." I slumped on the love seat to the side of her desk and she swiveled to look at me, taking her reading glasses off and letting them hang from their chain. That's how I always know she's listening to me. I lay down, feeling like I was at a psychiatrist's office.

"Why?" she asked.

"Well, Hailey and Jenna are together all the time now because they're taking this 'watercolor' class and they have to do their 'homework.'" I made little quotation marks in the air in disgust.

"That doesn't sound too awful," she said.

I could tell my mom was smiling, and I didn't even have to look at her to confirm it; I could hear it in her voice.

"It's not funny."

"I know. Sorry. It was the quotation marks. So you feel left out because they have this new thing together?"

"Yes." I pouted.

"And would you want to take that class too?" she asked.

Actually, I hadn't thought of it. Maybe because no one had even asked! But to be honest, the answer was no. "No," I said.

"So is there something you miss doing with Hailey?" she asked.

"Well . . . lately we'd mostly been doing homework together."

"Hmm," said my mom.

"What does 'hmm' mean?" I asked, doing the quotation marks again.

"'Hmm' means maybe Hailey was getting tired of being with someone who's always better than her at something."

I thought about that for a minute; then I thought about what Hailey had said about being good at watercolors. "Well," I said.

"And maybe she was tired of needing help from you."

"She's the one who asks for it!" I sputtered.

"Maybe. But maybe you two have gotten into a bit of a rut," said my mom. "What do you like to do with Hailey?"

"Have sleepovers. Go to the movies. Talk."

"Okay," said my mom.

"Okay what?"

"Call her up! Invite her for a sleepover! I'll take you to the movies!"

"Take us?" I was indignant.

"Fine! Drop you off at the movies!"

I was quiet for a minute as I considered it. Then I said, "Fine." I knew I was being a little bratty, but it was also kind of funny. I liked that the solution might be that easy too.

We were quiet for another moment.

"And Michael?" my mother asked gently.

I sighed heavily. "I never see him. Or not that much. And it's like, are we only friends because Mr. Trigg assigns us to be? Or would we be friends otherwise?"

"What do you think?" asked my mom.

"I think we're friends. But it's weird, because if we don't have an article to work on, then we don't have an excuse to hang out. But if I ask him to hang out, because he's a boy, it's kind of like asking him on a date."

"Hmm. Do you think he'd see it that way?" my mom asked.

"Yes, definitely!"

"And would that be bad?"

"Yes! Definitely!"

"Okay, so what's he busy with now that you two aren't working together?"

"I told you the other day. Writing the article with that British girl Kate!"

"Oh. Right. Well. Is she nice?"

"She's okay, but I think she wants my life. First she steals my job, then my crush, and now she wants my future, too."

My mom laughed, and I turned to glare at her. "Sorry," she said. "But what's your future?"

"Editor in chief. She said her mom wants her to go for it. And you know that's my dream."

"Hmm. But did she say she wants it?" asked my mom.

"Noooo . . . but come on! Who wouldn't want editor in chief?"

"Lots of people," said my mom. "It's a lot of work, and on top of your regular course load and any other extracurriculars you might do. Is she busy?"

I cringed a little, thinking of my eavesdropping. "Yes," I said quietly.

"Well, then, she might not want it, despite the fact that you do. And why do you think she likes Michael? I mean as more than just a cowriter?"

I shrugged.

"Has she said anything about him being cute, or does she get giggly around him?" asked my mom.

"No," I said quietly.

"Hmm," said my mom again. And then, "You know, sometimes when there's something we really like or something we really want, we assume that the rest of the world must want it too. But that's not always the case. You'd be surprised. Maybe Kate likes skinny guys with glasses! Who knows?"

I laughed, and so did my mom.

"Does she have any other friends yet?" she asked.

"I don't know," I said. "Actually, I don't think so."

"Is she nice to you?" my mom asked.

I hated to admit it. "Yes," I said quietly.

"Do you think she could be a friend one day, if you weren't competitors?"

I didn't say anything.

"Samantha?"

"Yes. Fine, yes."

"Why?"

"I don't know. We both like the news and writing. She's funny and nice." I hated to admit it.

"Do you think Kate could use a friend?"

"Whatever. Yes."

My mom was quiet for a minute, and I turned to look at her. "What?"

"I think you need to make three different plans with three different people. I can help you think them up, if you like, and I can handle the funds and transportation." My mom was grinning.

"Maybe for Kate and Hailey. But the Michael thing: no. Just not happening."

"Whatever you say," said my mom. "Maybe

there's another way to let him know you miss him, though."

"Humph," I said. I couldn't think of any.

★　　★　　★

The next day I went into high gear for my uniforms article. One thing about me is that I am never afraid to pick up the phone and make a call, especially if it's for an article. Face-to-face meetings are something else, but the phone is my friend. It calms me down.

So I called the principal's office and I booked an interview with Mr. Pfeiffer, the principal, later that afternoon. (I was terrified since I've always interviewed him with Michael at my side; I considered asking if it could be a phone interview, but that seemed weird, since we spend all day in the same building.)

Then I Googled a school uniform company and got the marketing director on the phone and was able to get some great quotes both for and against the wearing of uniforms in school. She also said she'd overnight me a bunch of materials, catalogues and stuff to look at, and an e-mail with links to studies that have been done showing how great uniforms can be in a school setting.

I also called Father Powers, the head of the parochial school in our town, and talked to him on the phone about school uniforms, since they have them at his school. He was very for them, since he sees them as "lessening outside distractions in a school setting" and "equalizing the economic playing field," but he pointed out that it was very time-consuming for faculty and administration to enforce the dress code. That was a pretty good point. You'd have to have a system in place to deal with infractions, and I'm not sure we needed more things we could get punished for in school.

Online, I found a really good quotation from former President Clinton about school uniforms, which would go in the "pro" side of the argument. To be honest, I was mostly having a hard time finding information against school uniforms. After all, if the great Allie Martone, fashion fiend of the century, is *for* school uniforms, who could be against them?

Chapter 7

PEACE TALKS THAW DIPLOMATIC FREEZE

★ ★ ★

The principal, as it turned out. That's who was against uniforms.

I was practically shaking as I waited my turn outside Mr. Pfeiffer's office. Michael and I had had a couple of run-ins with him doing interviews, and I wasn't his favorite student, that's for sure. Kids coming and going to see the vice principal (in charge of discipline) gave me oddly pitying looks on the sofa, assuming I'd done something so bad I had to see the head honcho. It was embarrassing.

When Mr. Pfeiffer came to the door to call me in, I managed a weak smile and a firm handshake (hoping he wouldn't notice my hands were like ice cubes, which is what happens when I'm nervous).

"Ms. Martone, always a pleasure," he said, though I didn't really believe him. Mr. Pfeiffer is a pretty good guy and actually a really good principal, but there was no love lost between us.

"So we're here today about school uniforms?" he said. He's always pretty prepared, so I wasn't surprised that he was ready for me.

"Yes, sir. Mr. Trigg assigned the topic just as an exploration. I've been asking around and looking to hear from people who are for or against it, and what their reasons are." I pulled out my notebook and pen and sat ready to jot down Mr. Pfeiffer's list of pros and quotes about why the PTA always gave him a hard time about adopting uniforms, but that wasn't how it turned out at all.

"Well, Ms. Martone, you might be surprised to know I'm one of the only principals around who is not *for* uniforms in our school."

My jaw must've dropped because he laughed.

"I know." He continued. "Surprising. But let me tell you why. Certainly I can see all the pros, and I know all the arguments well. I do think uniforms are an equalizer of sorts. However, I would argue that it is still obvious—sometimes more painfully so—what the cliques are and who the rich and poor are, even *with* uniforms. Uniforms are easily tweaked—skirts shortened, sleeves rolled, pants worn low, accessories added to within a millimeter of the guidelines—and I think that kids, especially tweens and teens—are able to make uniforms their own in a very distinct way. It almost becomes a challenge for them. *How far can I go and still be in dress code?* I am not interested in policing clothing any more than we already do."

My pen flew over the pages of my notebook, filling the lines with his surprising words.

"I don't think that uniforms are more economical for families, as the rich family that buys the designer shoes will still buy the designer shoes, and the poor family that has little to spend will still stretch to afford the uniforms; only now they'll need those in addition to weekend clothes.

"But here's the crux of it for me: If we do not teach our kids from a young age how to deal with the differences in life—economic, stylistic, self-expressionistic—then when will they learn to deal with them? How can we tell kids it's important to look beyond the surface when we're trying to make the surface all the same?"

"Hmm," I said. He had a point. A good one.

"I think differences in style, taste, clothing, and self-expression are something kids should learn to live with, work with, and move beyond. And that's why I am against uniforms in schools."

"Okay," I said, still writing. I finished the last sentence and then I looked up. He was smiling at me. It startled me, and I guess it showed on my face.

"Not what you expected, eh?"

I had to laugh. "Not at all."

"Do you think the students will be pleased or disappointed to hear my opinion on this?"

I thought for a moment. "Probably pleased, though more of them are for it than against, judging from my random sampling. Or, I should say, if they're not actually for it, they wouldn't be totally against it."

"Well put," said Mr. Pfeiffer.

"Have you had any pressure from the community to adopt uniforms?" I asked.

"No," he said.

I glanced at my list of questions. "What about from the superintendent of schools or other governmental bodies or officials?"

"No. They distribute the research, but there is no pressure."

I had one question left. "Did you have to wear a uniform as a child?" I smiled.

"Yes," said Mr. Pfeiffer with a laugh. "And I swore I'd never do it again!"

"Aha!" I said.

"Aha!" he echoed, and we laughed.

Too much laughter in an interview usually means you're not asking tough enough questions; I've learned that the hard way. Was there something I should be asking that I hadn't thought of? Totally off the cuff, I asked, "Do you think there's a gender divide when it comes to school attire that would be corrected by uniforms?"

Mr. Pfeiffer was thoughtful for a moment, and then he said, "If you're asking if the female students spend more time thinking about what they're going to wear, then my cautious answer is yes, but it's only because there are so many more options for them. I think many of the boys *care* just as much what their clothing says about them. I just think they have fewer choices to work with."

"Good observation," I said, writing it down.

"Yes, well, we've had quite a lot of gender-blindness training around here, and I wouldn't presume to know what someone's thinking until I'd walked a mile in her shoes—whether they're UGGS or sneakers or flats." There was that expression again! I laughed again. "Well, thank you very much for your time, Mr. Pfeiffer. I think there will be a lot of relieved kids out there."

"Thank you for contacting me for my opinion. I do like to be asked! And thanks for covering the topic. It's a good one."

We shook hands and I left for lunch.

★　　★　　★

On line in the cafeteria, I played a little game with myself where I tried to guess who was friends with whom based on their clothing, or whether kids were rich or poor, or "cool." I decided it had as much to do with clothes as it did with makeup, hairstyle, accessories, shoes, and book bags as with anything else. Uniforms probably wouldn't be the great equalizer people make them out to be. I got my soup and half a bagel with cream cheese and was looking for a seat when I felt a tap on my shoulder.

"Hi!"

It was Kate with her tray. My heart sank a little.

"Hey," I said.

"Looking for company?" she asked.

"Sure," I said. I tried to channel what my mom had said about Kate maybe not being interested in being editor in chief and maybe not being interested in Michael. It kind of worked.

I looked around for Hailey but didn't see her, so we sat near the window in an area where I don't usually sit and began chatting and eating. We got into talking about our favorite writers and the best books we'd ever read . . . something I never discuss with Hailey or even Michael, despite the fact that he's a words guy. It felt great to realize we had a lot of the same tastes, and we exchanged e-mail addresses because Kate promised to e-mail me a list of the books she'd

loved in the past year. She actually keeps a list of
every book she's ever read (I hope she doesn't tell
Michael that, because then he'll start calling her
Listy too and I'll be jealous!). We decided that if
we had time after lunch, we'd stop by the library
and pick out some books, just for pleasure reading. I was psyched.

We were having such a good time that it wasn't
until we stood to leave that I spotted Hailey eating
in another corner of the cafeteria all by herself.

I crossed the room quickly, calling, "Hails!"
as I walked.

She looked up, but she didn't smile. She was
just starting her lunch.

"Hey, why didn't you sit with us?" I asked in
surprise as Kate drew up behind me.

Hailey shrugged. "You guys were engrossed. I
didn't want to interrupt."

"Are you nuts, Jones?" I said. "Interrupt?"

"Whatever," she said. It seemed like she was
mad at me.

I put my tray down. "We can sit with you now,
if you like? I still have ten minutes till my next

class," I said, conveniently forgetting about going to the library with Kate.

"No, I'm fine. I have to study. I have a quiz after this." She reached down and brought up a workbook.

"Want me to quiz you?" I offered. Usually we would have studied together.

"That's okay," she said.

Behind me, Kate said, "Girls, I'll leave you to it. I've got to go choose a book for later. See you soon, I hope!" And she left.

I felt torn. I would have loved to go to the library with Kate and look at books, make comments and recommendations, chat about writing. But I could hardly walk away from my best friend eating lunch alone in the cafeteria.

"Bye, Kate," I called after her, feeling like a traitor all around.

I sighed heavily.

"You don't have to stay," said Hailey.

I looked at her. "I want to. I . . . I miss you," I said.

Hailey melted. "I miss you, too! I feel like

we never see each other anymore!"

"I know. It was like we got into this rut of doing only homework together and that wasn't fun. And then you've been spending time with Jenna, and I've been jealous, and . . ."

"I know. And now you're besties with Kate," added Hailey, looking away.

"What?" I sputtered, disbelieving. "Are you kidding?"

Hailey looked back at me and grinned. "Yes."

I fake whacked her with a napkin. "You got me, you jerk."

"Busted. She isn't bad, though, right? I do like her. I think you'll be friends when all this newspaper stuff blows over."

"I hope so," I admitted. "Not *best* friends, of course. That job is filled. Meanwhile, my mother has invited you to the movies and a sleepover. When can you come?" I asked with a grin.

Hailey laughed. "Just your mother? Thanks a lot, Sam."

"And me too, of course. And probably Allie, since she does love to have her fans around at all times. Are you free this weekend?" I asked.

"Yes, for sure. I have an outing Saturday for my class, but I *am* free tonight or late Saturday."

"Let's do it tonight, then," I said, happy to have a weekend plan.

"I'm glad you admitted you miss me," said Hailey.

"I lied," I said with a grin and a wink. ***Peace Talks Thaw Diplomatic Freeze.***

When I got home, I e-mailed Kate. It said:

R u free Saturday afternoon? Want to go to Starbucks n bookstore? LMK!

It wasn't even a minute before she replied.

Y! Can't wait! Thanks for asking!

Good old Mom. She did give good advice, I had to admit. Conveniently, I pushed out of my mind her advice to invite one last person to do something. That was just not going to happen.

Chapter 8

SELF-INFLICTED INJURIES LEADING CAUSE OF DEATHS IN THE WORKPLACE

★ ★ ★

I was walking at full speed, on my way for one last check of the Dear Know-It-All box before I picked a letter and drafted a reply over the weekend, when I crashed into Michael Lawrence, who was coming the other way.

"Whoa!" he said, steadying himself against the wall.

I slipped a little and banged my elbow against the molding on the wall.

"Ow!" I said, cradling my throbbing elbow. *Self-Inflicted Injuries Leading Cause of Deaths in the Workplace.*

Michael laughed. "I should have known. It's been about a full week since you've hurt me or done something klutzy in front of me, Pasty. We were overdue."

"Very funny, not!" I said. "Ouch!" I moaned again.

Michael was grinning at me.

"What?" I asked.

"Nothing. I haven't seen you in ages," he said.

"Really?" I asked. I was being defensive, since I knew exactly how long it had been, but when I saw the hurt look in his eyes I quickly realized I'd been too tough, bordering on rude, so I changed my tune. "I mean, I know! I noticed that too!" I wanted to add that I was surprised he had noticed since he'd been so busy with Miss United Kingdom, but I bit my tongue (not literally!).

"What's up with you?" he asked.

"Not much. You?" I already knew the answer but had to ask out of politeness.

"Just working. School, practice, and the paper. I miss—" But he stopped himself.

"What?" I asked. *Please say me! Please say me!* I was thinking it so hard I almost thought he could hear me.

"I miss your work ethic," he said.

Oh.

"Thanks, I guess," I said, deflating.

There was a tiny pause. "Anything you miss about me?" he prompted.

"Oh. Um. Your cinnamon buns?" I joked. Michael happens to make the best cinnamon buns in the world.

"That's all?" He pretended to be wounded and staggered a little.

I laughed. "No. I miss your steel-trap memory, too. I interviewed Pfeiffer this morning and it was a doozy! I wished I didn't have to write everything down."

Michael was excited. "You interviewed him alone? How did it go? What was it about?"

"The school uniforms debate. He was very interesting about it, actually."

"Wow, Paste. I can't believe you dialed that guy up and just marched on in there all by yourself. Way to go!" We grinned at each other, and then he said casually, "So how is it working alone?"

"Oh, it's . . ." I was going to fake it and say

"great," but that was mean, and it was actually the opposite of the truth. "It's lonely," I said, shrugging. "I miss having a partner."

Michael smiled. "That's too bad," he said.

"Then why are you smiling?" I asked. I couldn't believe I'd actually said that aloud.

"Oh, just thinking."

"How is it with, uh, Kate Bigley?" I asked.

Michael's brows knit together the way they always do when he's searching for the right thing to say. I gulped while I waited, wishing I'd never asked. Finally he said, "Uh, let's just say you two have very different approaches to journalism."

"That's all?" I pressed.

"Pretty much all I can say at this point," he said, looking away.

"Is it going well?" I asked. I'm a fool. Why did I even want to know?

"Oh, yeah. Sure. It's going pretty well," he said. But he wouldn't look me in the eye!

Either this guy was in love with Kate Bigley, or things were going terribly. I couldn't tell, and it was going to drive me crazy.

"Okay. Any big weekend plans?" I asked. I had to know if he was going out with her or something.

"Nah," he said. "It's Jeff's birthday, so his mom is taking us to paintball on Saturday."

"Fun!" I said. It actually sounded like torture to me, but I know boys love that sort of thing.

"Yeah! Anyway, that's about all. So . . ."

"Yeah. So. I need to get going to class. So bye!"

"Oh, okay. Bye," he said. But I walked away first.

I don't know why, but I was confused and kind of sad as I walked away. I felt like there was so much being unsaid, and from his side I couldn't tell if it was good or bad.

In the newsroom there were lots of other kids working on stories, so I couldn't look for new Dear Know-It-All letters. I'd e-mail Mr. Trigg and ask him to check for me later. I hoped there'd be something superjuicy for me. If nothing else had come in, I'd have to go with what I had, since I'd need to write the reply on Sunday in order to hand it in on time next week. None of the choices were that great, but I'd have to make do. I was looking forward to Sunday, actually, because I had a lot of parts of the school uniforms article. On Sunday I'd tie it all together in a draft, then finalize it on Monday. I was also looking forward to the sleepover with Hailey. She could set up a survey on Buddybook for me tonight to poll who was for and who was against the idea. I always like going to the people on things like this, even if it is a little skewed toward those who favor social media.

★　★　★

After school my mom took me and Hailey to the grocery store to get stuff for Make Your Own Sundaes. We were going to get pizza at the mall and then see the movie and have dessert at home later. My mom refuses to pay movie theater snack prices. We got all kinds of awesome toppings: crispy chocolate shell, dulce de leche, marshmallow cream, waffle cookies to crumble over the top, and three flavors of ice cream. Hailey was in junk-food heaven since her mom is a health nut. As we piled the stuff in the basket, we howled with laughter at the possible combinations, jokingly pointing to other stuff on the shelves that we could add and making up funny sundae names. My mom was just shaking her head at us, smiling, as we reached the end of the aisle to get on line, when who should we see up ahead but Kate Bigley!

She was heading toward the checkout line with her own mom, and we called out to her. She smiled and waved, so we went to stand behind her and there were introductions all around. Her mom was pretty and chic, in very trim, fitted clothes that were simple but stylish. She and my mom chatted while we showed Kate all the junk food we'd bought, but I was feeling terribly guilty. I wished there was a way I could have a telepathic conversation with Hailey that Kate couldn't hear. I wanted to say, *I feel bad for Kate and feel like we should invite her, but I don't want to share my special evening with you with her, too!* I thought about the shoe being on the other foot (shoes again!), and how I'd feel if I were Kate, and that's when I decided to invite her. Only, to my surprise, Hailey beat me to it.

"Hey, why don't you come with us? You could

come to Sam's, then the movie, and sleep over afterward with us!"

Kate's eyes lit up at the invitation. Hailey looked questioningly at me to see if I was on board and I nodded. "Yes, please come! It will be fun!"

"Oh, that's so sweet of you," said Kate. "And I wish I could, but my parents are having some dinner guests I'd really like to meet, so I've got to stay home, you see?"

"Ooh! Who are they?" asked Hailey as I stared daggers at her. She can be sort of clueless, like not realizing it's sort of an impolite thing to ask someone that.

"Well, it's . . . my mom's actually a writer, and it's her editor and his wife, who's an agent. I think they're neat because they know all sorts of famous literary people and they like to talk books all night long and gossip about authors!"

"Wow!" I breathed. I couldn't imagine a night like that. "That's so cool that your mom is a writer. What does she write?"

"Oh, fiction. Short stories. She's had a novel published. She writes for British *Vogue* sometimes and *Tatler*, which is a magazine back home."

"That's so cool! How come you never said so?" I asked. I was actually kind of hurt that she hadn't shared that with me at lunch the other day, or ever.

Kate shrugged. "It's . . . I don't know. It's her gig, you know?"

"Is she famous?" asked Hailey, her eyes agog.

Kate laughed. "To a very small group of people, yes."

"Wow. Cool," said Hailey. "I can't imagine wanting to write."

"Hailey, come on!" I said.

"Ready, girls?" asked my mom. "Is Kate coming along?"

"Thanks, Mrs. Martone, but I'm going to stay home tonight. Sam and I have plans for tomorrow, though. Have fun, girls!"

"You too! Take notes!" I said.

"Ugh! Notes! My least favorite thing about journalism!" Kate laughed. "Besides research!" She laughed again.

"Bye!" we said.

Outside, Hailey and I were quiet as we put the

bags in the car and climbed in. After a minute, my mom laughed. "Cat got your tongues back there, girls?"

I realized it was quiet. "No. I was just thinking. It's weird that Kate hates notes and research and she's a journalist, right?"

"Why?" asked Hailey. "I hate them, too."

"Because those are like two of the main things about being a journalist, along with interviewing people and writing. That's pretty much it. It's just weird that you'd hate fifty percent of what you do."

"Some people hate more than that," said my mom. "And they get up and go to jobs all day long where they hate seventy-five, eighty, one hundred percent of what they do."

"That would stink," I said.

"Yeah," agreed Hailey. "Almost as much as having a friend who makes all kinds of plans with other people without telling you."

"What? Hails! Come on!" I laughed. "Are you mad I'm doing something with Kate tomorrow?"

My mom turned up the radio to give us some privacy, and she began singing along, loudly and with the wrong words. I cringed and wished Hailey weren't mad right now so we could share a look and giggle about my mom. *Insane Mom Thinks She's Hip: Top 40 Her Ticket to Loony Bin.*

But Hailey shrugged and looked out the window silently for a moment.

"I asked you first!" I protested.

"You just have so much more in common with her," said Hailey. "I just know you're going to end up liking her more and dump me."

I swatted her. "Don't be ridiculous! No one could ever replace you! And anyway, how do you think I feel with you hanging out with Jenna all the time?"

"I only started hanging out with Jenna because you were with Michael all the time," said Hailey.

I wanted to giggle at the expression "got Jenna," but I knew it wasn't the right time. It would only make Hailey madder. She gets self-conscious if she thinks I'm teasing her for being dumb (which she isn't and I never do). "Well, as long as we each know we come first," I said.

"Deal?" I put out my hand for her to shake.

She looked down at it like she wasn't going to take it; then she quickly spit into her palm and held it out to me.

"Eeeewww!" I screamed, slapping her hand away, and just like that, we were back. If only it were that easy with Michael.

Chapter 9

ALLIANCES SHIFT AS NEW BATTLE LINES ARE DRAWN!

★ ★ ★

Hailey and I had a blast at the mall. Pizza was fun: We ran into a bunch of girls we're friends with from school, and we all sat together and checked out some accessories they'd bought with their babysitting money.

The movie was good. It was a romantic comedy, and everything about the couple reminded me of me and Michael. I cried when they broke up and cried when they got back together and all around loved it.

Back home we chowed our sundaes—even Allie and my mom made their own—and then we headed upstairs to "settle in," as my mom calls it. But we weren't going to settle immediately.

There was a Buddybook survey to set up first. We got in our pj's and brushed our teeth; then Hailey pulled up her page and helped set up a little poll for me. It basically asked if kids were for or against school uniforms. We didn't make it specific to Cherry Valley Middle School, since it would be too hard to control for the answers, and anyway, since it wasn't up for real as a possibility, it didn't even matter. Hailey said she'd check it again for me tomorrow morning and tomorrow night, and I'd run with whatever the final tally was tomorrow night.

After Hailey did that, we decided we'd better look at Michael Lawrence's page. He doesn't have a photo up of himself—just a photo of his dog, Humphrey, who is a basset hound and really cute; even his dog is cute!—but a lot of times people tag him and their photos appear on his page. As we poked around his wall, Hailey suddenly gasped and pointed. I looked closely, and it was a tiny photo of Kate Bigley: her profile picture next to her name. She and Michael Lawrence were Buddybook friends! And not only that, they were playing an ongoing game of Words with Pals!

Alliances Shift as New Battle Lines Are Drawn!

Hailey and I looked at each other in shock; then I dropped my face in my hands and wailed. "I knew it! I knew they'd end up together! This is just like in the movie tonight when the guy meets the new girl!"

"Okay," said Hailey, trying to click on the link to read the thread of the game, but it was locked. "Listen." She grabbed me by the shoulders and made me look at her. "Just because they're playing some kind of dorky online Scrabble thingy doesn't mean they're dating." Then Hailey muttered, "Why anyone would waste their time practicing their spelling online is beyond me. . . ."

I had to laugh. "It's not just spelling, Hails!"

"Oh, whatever! You know what I mean. Let's look at her page and see who she knows, okay?"

Hailey did some clicking and we were on Kate's page, but it was locked.

"Should I send her a buddy request?" asked Hailey.

I thought about it for a minute. "Nah. Not

tonight. I'm not in the mood to know any more anyway."

"O-kayy . . . ," said Hailey. "But if you change your mind . . ."

"Okay, I changed my mind. But you know what? Send it tomorrow after you leave. She knows you're sleeping over, and it'll look like we were Buddybooking all night long, checking her out and stuff."

Hailey looked at me. "But we are."

"Duh!" I laughed. "But she doesn't need to know that."

We tried Googling her next, but nothing came up, except about some Kate Bigleys who were obviously older and not her.

"Whatever. This is boring." I looked at the clock. An hour had passed. "And a total time suck, as usual. Will you please check the survey before you log out?" I asked.

Hailey checked. "Wow. Already a lot of replies. Seventy-three for it, twenty-two against."

"Huh. It's totally weird, Hailey, but that's about the ratio I got when I interviewed people outside school the other day."

"Should we tack on a question about what the uniform should be?" asked Hailey, squinting at the comments on the screen.

"Nah. Thanks, though. With Pfeiffer's take on it all, I don't think anything will come of it anyway. Why make extra work for ourselves?" I said.

Hailey shut down the computer, saying, "You don't have to tell me twice."

After we got into our beds and turned out the lights, everything was quiet, and then Hailey said, "Sam? If you like Michael, why don't you just tell him? There's always all these misunderstandings between you two, and it's because you don't talk! For journalists, you're not very good at communicating."

"Maybe I should write it down." I yawned. There was no way I was going to tell him anything of the sort.

★　　★　　★

Hailey left early for her watercolor field trip the next morning, but not without checking Buddybook for me.

"First of all, Michael hasn't replied on Words with Pals, just FYI."

"Thanks. That is the important news, after all."

"Second of all, the current polls are in and it's two hundred and thirty-four for to fifty-nine against uniforms."

"Wow! People really have no life!"

"I know. It's sad."

"Imagine the losers who *write* these polls," I said, grinning.

"They must be total dweebs," agreed Hailey, laughing.

"Have fun today, Hails," I said, standing up and giving her a big hug in her chair.

After she left, I had some time to look at the Dear Know-It-All letters again. Mr. Trigg had e-mailed me back last night to say that there weren't any more letters so I'd better just go with something I had, assuming there was something good enough.

Sadly, there was something good *enough*, but it wasn't what I needed. I needed better than good enough. I needed awesome! I decided I'd go with the

"I miss my friend" letter, since it hit home the most for me. I started mapping out my reply, listing all kinds of things I could suggest they do together, like "Take a class," "Go paint pottery together," "Play Words with Pals" (aaargh!), and more. I'd write a little about the importance of shared interests and how they could keep friends united, and about making an effort to plan social outings and sleepovers and stuff. I had quite a lot of material by the time I'd completed my brainstorming, and I knew I could keep coming up with more. This column would be a blockbuster. A friendship 101 guidebook (or guide column—I was getting carried away!).

When I finished, an hour had passed and it was time for me to go meet Kate at the mall. Where before I'd been really looking forward to our outing, now I was kind of dreading it. I knew the subject of Michael would come up. How could it not? But what would I say? Ugh. I had a stomachache just thinking about it.

★ ★ ★

"Sam!"

I turned to see Kate waving heartily at me from

the Starbucks at the end of the mall.

"Hey!" I called in reply, and picked up my pace to meet her.

She started chatting as soon as I was within earshot. "Oh, I was so nervous you wouldn't come! New-girl jitters and all that. Like maybe I'd misunderstood, or gotten the time wrong or something."

"Am I late?" I asked, feeling bad suddenly. I looked at my watch. Three minutes to spare.

"No, I'm just pathetically early because I had nothing else to do."

"Oh, what did you get?"

"A strawberry Frappuccino and a cupcake. It's divine right now, but I'll probably feel ghastly once I've finished it." Kate grinned. "It's a lot of sugar!"

"I'll get the same." I went to order while she saved a seat for me at the counter that paralleled the line. While I waited, I saw a girl from my homeroom and we waved at each other; then my friend Tricia's mom walked by and we said hello. Finally the barista was the girl who's always there on the weekends, which is the only time I go, and she knows my name because they need it to write on the cups for our orders. I know hers (Tara) because she wears it on her name tag. We greeted each other by name and had a little chat about the weather or whatever, and after she gave me my change, I went to perch on the stool next to Kate until they called my name.

"You must know everyone *in* here!" Kate exclaimed as I sat down.

"What? No, not really," I said.

"It seems like it. This is really your hometown. You're lucky."

"I'm sure it would be the same for you in your hometown," I offered generously, but Kate shook her head.

"No. We've moved three times in the past four years. My mom is trying to get a teaching post at a university, and if you're not offered tenure after the first year, you move on. So now I never know anyone anywhere."

"Bummer," I said. "Or maybe it's really freeing? You can do whatever you want, wear whatever you want, and no one will hold you back or call you out on it."

"I guess. I just miss my old friends. And a few recent new ones, too."

"Oh, do you keep in touch?" I asked, thinking of Buddybook.

"A little, on Buddybook." She paused. Then she said, "Hey, how come you're not on it?"

`I was surprised. "How did you know?" I asked. And, of course, right then they called me for my Frappuccino. "Hang on." I got it and came back.

"Because I tried to buddy you and you don't exist there. I wanted to play Words with Pals with you, once I knew you were a wordie like me."

Aha. And like Michael Lawrence, obviously!

"Oh. So . . . um, who do you play with?" I asked.

"I play mostly with my pals from home. Though I started a game with Michael Lawrence, and he never makes his moves. It's awfully frustrating, but then I shouldn't be surprised."

"Oh?" Every nerve in my body thrummed as I waited for more information from her. "Why?"

Kate sighed in exasperation. "He's probably working too hard to bother with a silly thing like that. He's such a perfectionist! Always wanting us to check every little fact, do more research, call one more person. He's kind of a tyrant. I don't know how you put up with him," she said. "Oh, but actually I do. Because you're perfect!"

"What? Me?" I nearly choked on my Frappuccino. The last word I'd even use to describe myself would be "perfect."

"Yes, *you*, Sam Martone!" Kate said, smiling. "According to Michael Lawrence, anyway."

"Oh, stop. No way," I said. "I drive him crazy." But I was tingling inside.

"You certainly do, but not in the way you mean." She laughed. "He's always scolding me. 'That's not the way Sam does this,' or 'Sam always gets the quotes right the first time,' or 'One time Sam said . . .' and on and on. Oh, my word! If I didn't feel secure in myself and my writing, I'd just about drop to the floor in a heap, listening to him natter on about you!" She laughed again, shaking her head.

"Ha-ha," I tittered nervously. Was this for real?

"Yes, it's been very difficult for me to step into the Martone shoes in the famous Martone/Lawrence team. Like being an understudy. An insufficient one at best. I can't wait until it's over. I wish Mr. Trigg had never asked me to do it. It's just not playing to my strengths."

I was so overjoyed at the compliments she was passing along that I could hardly participate in the conversation, but I made a huge effort and asked, "What are your strengths?"

"Oh, I love writing about fashion and pop culture. And my actual writing is pretty great, if I do say so myself."

I had to smile, thinking of what I'd said to Hailey about my own writing, just a week earlier. But I didn't see this as a brag. When a reporter dissects her own skills like this, she's probably giving herself a pretty fair evaluation.

"Wow. So you should be writing the school uniforms piece and I should be writing the year-round-school article. Is that right?" I joked.

But Kate was dead serious. "Yes. Though I

would write the uniform article as a fashion piece with lots of photos of kids in uniforms and how they accessorize them to look great. We could have tons of photos from that guy. . . . What's his name? The friend of Michael's?"

"Jeff Perry?" I said. It was funny she didn't even know Michael's best friend's name. She and Michael couldn't be spending much time together if she didn't know *that*, at least.

"Yes! He would make a fabulous fashion photographer."

I giggled, picturing Jeff Perry hanging out with a bunch of models, or even a gaggle of pretty girls. He'd eat it up! I was feeling better by the minute about all of this. But I didn't want to get too relaxed in case she had her eye on Michael for the future.

"So do you think Michael's cute?" I asked.

She paused, thoughtful. "Well, I wouldn't even bother to think about it, seeing as how he's so smitten with you. But since you ask, I do have a sort of boyfriend back home and—no offense—but he's more my type. I really like blond guys. Athletic . . .

not so much, you know? More the poet type."

I laughed out loud and Kate blushed. "Is that just gross to you?" she asked. "Am I totally off the American girl's taste?"

"Oh my gosh, sorry. No! Not at all. I just . . . Oh, I guess I'm relieved. . . ." I couldn't believe I'd admitted it to her, but she'd been so honest, so open and forthright with me all along, I could see now that I owed her the same. Because suddenly I knew Kate Bigley and I were going to be very good friends for a very long time (even if I ended up having to join Buddybook to stay in touch with her). And since that was the case, it was time to come clean with her. "See, here's the thing . . . ," I said. And as we sat on our uncomfortable bar stools at the Starbucks in the mall, I told her the whole story about Michael.

Chapter 10

NUCLEAR WINTER THAWS AS TALKS CONTINUE

★ ★ ★

Kate and I spent a really fun afternoon together, never running out of things to talk about. She loved the Michael Lawrence crush story, even the Pasty part, and she was mortified at her role in separating me from my one true love. She even offered to step down from the article so I could finish it with Michael, but there was no way I'd take her up on that. First of all, it would look bad for her, and second of all, there was no way I was taking on all that work at this late stage in the issue! She swore he only talked about me, and she wanted to talk about ways to get us together. I laughed because that's what Hailey is always trying to do, too.

At the bookstore Kate introduced me to the

work of John Green, which she said is amazing, and I told her about Lauren Myracle, whose books I really like. We both loved the Dork Diaries and had read all the books in the series, and we went over all the recent bestsellers and said what we thought of the ones we'd read. I could spend all day in the bookstore, the same way my mom could spend all day in the hardware store. I guess it's all about being surrounded by what excites you and shows you the most possibility.

Kate told me all about the dinner with her parents and their friends the night before. She also told me about a bestselling author of adult books who we both like to read when our parents aren't looking, and how the woman has nine children and writes for a week straight sometimes, having her meals delivered and showering in her office bathroom.

I told Kate how I really want to be a journalist when I grow up and travel to scary places to uncover the truth.

"I have no doubt you will do that, Sam," said Kate, and it felt great hearing it from her.

When it was time to go meet our moms, we didn't want to leave, but we both were tired and had a lot of work to do at home. We hugged before we got into our cars and made a plan to do the same thing next week, maybe meeting Jenna and Hailey for lunch or a movie too. I was so excited to have made a new friend who shares so many of my interests, and I told my mom all about her and our day as we drove home.

"Did you know she's moved three times in the last four years?" I said. "And all her friends are back at the original place! But she still is in touch with all of them almost every day. Wow. I can't imagine how hard that is," I said, shaking my head in wonder.

My mother looked at me in the rearview mirror. "You know how much I hate to say 'I told you so,' right?" she said with a smile.

"Right." I nodded. "So I'll say it for you: You told me so."

"Thanks," said my mom. And she turned up the radio and started singing along.

★ ★ ★

Sunday morning I got up early and began pulling together all my uniform pieces and facts and figures. Hailey called in a tally of 567 for uniforms and 129 against them. We were really shocked.

I started writing at about ten o'clock, and by twelve I had a ten-page article that I really was starting to like. I stopped for lunch and then went back and edited it down to eight pages. I cut and pasted a few photos from the school uniform company's Website—a couple of funny vintage ones and a few current ones. They might want to run them with the article, so I'd gotten permission from the marketing director at the company in advance. I tacked the permission on to the article so the managing editor would have it on file if it ever came up. I took one last read though and then I decided to e-mail it to Kate for a fresh pair of eyes. First I IM'd her to see if she was there and willing to read it, and she was, both.

I sent it and then waited. I always hate that part, waiting for feedback. To distract myself, I did my homework (there wasn't much this weekend, thank goodness), and then I pulled up the Dear Know-It-All response to smooth that out.

But that just wasn't coming. I couldn't decide how to order the information and how to make it gender neutral. Like, should all the activity ideas be gender neutral ("Play Words with Pals"), which could get kind of boring, or should I separate the idea lists into one for girls and one for boys (like "Play paintball" and "Give each other mani-pedis")? This was obviously pretty sticky business and I'd really need Trigger's advice on it. I don't like sending things to an editor when they're not the very best I think they can be. But in this case, I really needed my editor's help, and since no one else but my mom knows I write this column, it would have to be Trigger.

I wrote up a little cover e-mail and attached my response. I was now ruining the surprise that I'd written a blockbuster, but at least he could start mentally mapping out the layout, now that he knew I'd be submitting a really long column for this issue.

Meanwhile, I had heard back from Kate!

Eagerly, I read her e-mail and looked for suggestions I could incorporate in any way, shape, or form. But I quickly saw she hadn't given me any notes. She wrote that it was "divine" and she gave many specific examples of things she'd liked and even loved, so I knew for sure she'd read it. But there was no constructive criticism to be found.

I wrote back. "Don't be shy, Kate. Any mistakes? Anything you'd change? Hate any parts? What's the most boring section, where your eyes truly glazed over?"

And then the phone rang. It was Kate. "I had to call. Honestly, it's flawless. I loved every inch of it, and I think you're a genius. I'm not just saying it. I swear!" Hmm. ***Nuclear Winter Thaws as Talks Continue.***

"Well . . . okay, I guess . . . ," I said skeptically. There had to be at least one typo. The odds were about a billion to one that there wasn't!

After we hung up, I sat and stared at my screen for a while. I couldn't swamp Trigger with my own insecurity, asking him to review everything I was working on. I had my reputation to maintain, after all. Hailey would be absolutely no help, and I felt too lazy to walk downstairs and ask my mom to read it.

Let's face it. There was only one person I wanted to hear from.

I typed up an e-mail apologizing for bothering him, and then I attached the document and hit send. I drummed my fingers on the table for a full five minutes while I waited for any sort of a reply. Then I gave up and went downstairs for a snack.

Since I was finished with my homework and in limbo on my articles, I settled in for an episode of *Star Dancing* with my mom and Allie and got totally sucked in. It was the perfect Sunday late-afternoon distraction.

When it was over, my mom stood up and stretched and went to get dinner going, while I hoped against hope that Michael had replied. I made myself climb the stairs slowly, cross my room slowly, lifted my screen slowly . . . and he had replied!

I sat on the edge of my seat and opened his e-mail. Which was long. Very long.

I began to read his comments and realized he had gone line by line to edit my article. Besides finding a bunch of typos and wrong word choices, as well as punctuation errors, Michael found an inconsistency I'd have to re-fact-check with the marketing company, a discrepancy in the wording of the Bill Clinton quote (having checked it against another source), and I'd carelessly said, "So we can see why Mr. Pfeiffer is for uniforms . . ." when I meant to say "against."

After I'd finished what Michael had written, I felt whipped. He had torn me apart and I hadn't been expecting it, especially after the lovefest with Kate earlier. Slowly, I began to get mad. I shut my computer and went down to dinner, where I barked at my mom, froze out Allie, and generally behaved badly (according to my mother). But when I explained what had made me so cranky, they took Michael's side!

"Sammy, you asked the guy for a critique! You *solicited* the criticism!" said Allie.

"Well, so? He didn't have to be so . . . thorough!" I said, knowing it sounded dumb and spoiled even

as the words left my mouth.

Allie rolled her eyes. "What, you want him to skip over errors just so you don't get mad at him?"

"No," I said, cutting my chicken. "But he didn't have to be so nitpicky."

"Oh, please!"

My mother watched us, amused.

"I'm glad you think it's funny!" I said finally.

"I do!" she said. "Here you have some really constructive help from a very close friend and writing partner, whom you greatly respect, who has taken a large chunk out of his own work time to slave over every word you've written to make it absolutely as perfect as can be. And you're mad at him! You two are really too much!" she said, shaking her head and laughing.

"Well," I huffed. "If you put it that way." And I finished my dinner, cleared my plate, and went upstairs to call Michael.

My fingers shook as I dialed the number (I know it by heart, of course), and luckily it was Michael himself who picked up on the second ring.

"Pasty!" he said happily.

"Michael," I said.

"Uh-oh," said Michael. "No Mikey? What have I done?"

"First of all, thank you for reading and . . . uh . . . fixing my article. I'm sure it will be greatly improved now that it has been under your eagle eye."

"Oh, so I was too aggressive, was I?" he asked, catching right on.

"Well, you certainly left no stone unturned," I agreed.

He sighed. "Listen, Paste. It's a great article. If no one had looked at it and you'd sent it in, I'm sure it would have been just fine. I just can't bear to see you, of all people, submit something that's less than perfect. It's just not right."

"Well, Kate read it and *she* thought it was perfect. She even used that word. *Perfect!*" I said indignantly.

Michael sighed loudly. "I'm not surprised," he said.

"What is that supposed to mean?" I asked haughtily.

Michael sighed again and then said, "Sam,

Kate is not a journalist. I'm not quite sure what she is, but she is definitely not a journalist. She doesn't like research. She doesn't like . . ."

"Notes," I offered.

"Right. Or, frankly, even facts. She doesn't like doing any of the hard work. She really just likes to write!" he said.

I giggled. "I know. She was really hoping for a fashion column. And instead she got the lead article with the meanest taskmaster in the school as her writing partner!"

"What?" Now Michael was the indignant one. "That's not fair! And it's not true! I'm not mean."

"No, I'm just teasing. She didn't say you were mean. But she did say it's hard work and very different from her paper back home."

"I know. I know. She tells me that all the time."

We were silent for a moment.

"So it needed that much work, huh? My little uniform article?"

"Little? That sucker was eight pages long!" cried Michael.

I grinned. "I know. I wrote it."

"Well, it wasn't up to your usual quality. That's all. And I hate to see your byline on something inferior to what you're capable of. You don't have to fix anything I said if you don't want to, obviously. It's a free country."

"Nah, I'll fix it. It's just annoying. You're right as usual."

"No, you're the one who's usually right around here," he teased.

"Oh, good thing I just got that on tape. I've been recording this whole conversation, in fact. I might just play it for one Kate Bigley . . . ," I joked.

"You'd better not, Pasty! I'll get you!" Michael said, laughing.

"Well, I'd better go. I've got *tons* of work to do on my article," I said.

"Hey, Paste? Thanks for asking me. Seriously. I was glad."

"Yeah. Anytime," I said. And we hung up, smiling. Both of us, I'm sure of it.

Chapter 11

JOURNALIST STRUCK BY CUPID'S ARROW DIES OF LOVE IN HALL

★ ★ ★

Mr. Trigg got back to me late Sunday night. He'd been at a World War II conference (his favorite topic) in Normandy, Michigan (for real), and he'd had no Wi-Fi on his flight to reply sooner.

But the gist of what he said was, *This is way too long of a reply to this lame letter.*

Why was everyone suddenly so down on my writing? I wondered. **Defeated Journalist Gets Kicked While Down.**

It didn't seem fair. But I made a mental note to stop by his office and catch him that day. It would be more efficient than a lot of e-mailing back and forth this close to deadline.

At school I ran into Kate and almost told her how Michael had ripped apart the article she had thought was "perfect," but I couldn't think of how to phrase it without making both of them look like jerks, so I just kept it to myself. I had lunch with Hailey, who had so loved her outdoor watercolor class on Saturday that she was planning another for this weekend, all with an eye toward doing an art show or even making a series of gift cards that she could sell to make money.

It was Michael whom I was most pleased to see, on my way to the news office. He walked me there, asking why I was going, and I made up some story about running something by Trigger before I sent the uniform article in to Susannah for editing.

We stopped just outside the newsroom, since Michael was on his way somewhere else. It felt good to be with him again, and I was glad the air was cleared about Kate, even though he'd never known it wasn't clear. But there was one nagging detail that was still bugging me. I had to know.

"So, Mikey, one question: Why didn't you tell me that you were having a hard time working with Kate?" I asked, shocked at my own nerve for asking and semidreading the answer.

Michael bit his lip, and his eyebrows knit together as he searched for the right words. "I guess . . . At first it was because I was giving her the benefit of the doubt. I just thought, you know, I couldn't presume to judge her, and if the shoe were on the other foot, I'd want to be given a fair chance to prove myself. Then, after a bit, I decided maybe there were cultural differences in the way we report things in our two countries. And finally I just decided she had no interest in doing the hard work. Which is fine, but I would have rather known sooner, so I could do it myself before the eleventh hour." He looked at me. "I guess I've gotten spoiled working with you, Pasty. You carry more than your fair share of the load."

"Whatever," I said, embarrassed again.

He was quiet for an extra second. "And really, most of all, I just didn't want you to think I couldn't do it without you, that I couldn't handle it."

"So you kept acting like everything was fine."

He looked at me. "Yeah."

"I wish you'd reached out earlier. I could have helped you," I said.

"I know. I won't ever do that again!" he joked.

"You're a stubborn one, Mr. Lawrence!"

"Well, Ms. Martone, if the shoe had been on the other foot . . . ," he said.

Why is everyone always talking about shoes around here?

"Good-bye, Mikey," I said, knowing I'd see him again soon.

Then I stepped into the newsroom and found Mr. Trigg blessedly alone in his office.

"Mr. Trigg?" I called. "Are you free?"

"Ah, Ms. Martone! How delightful to see you! Oh dear, am I allowed to say that?" he asked worriedly.

I laughed. "Yes. Compliments are always fine," I said. "As long as they're gender neutral."

"Good. Now, about the column . . ." He looked over his shoulder, shooed me into his office, and shut the door.

"Tea?" he asked, gesturing toward his electric teakettle.

"No, thanks," I said.

He began to whisper (Mr. Trigg loves all the

cloak-and-dagger aspects of the Dear Know-It-All column. I sometimes almost think that's why he keeps it on at the paper). "Ms. Martone. I think you've quite outdone yourself with this column."

"Outdone in a good way or a bad way?" I asked skeptically.

"Both," he whispered. "The writing is lovely, the brainstorming is excellent, but you've forgotten the most important question a good journalist must ask herself: Is it newsworthy?"

"Aha," I said, embarrassed.

"Do you think it is?" he asked.

I shook my head. "Not so much. I just . . . I wanted to do something splashy. But a splashy letter never came along, so I had to make the most of what I had."

"And why would *you*, of all people, need to be splashy?"

I didn't really know what to say, so I told the truth. "To stay on top." I shrugged.

Mr. Trigg sighed and dropped the whisper. "I've been chatting with Mr. Lawrence, and I can see I've made a dreadful mistake with this issue, Ms. Martone. Now, I don't want to get into specifics or criticize anyone's hard work. All our hearts are in the right place. But I am certain that I made an error when I allowed my sentimentality to overrule my intellect. I was spontaneous, when I should have been more measured and deliberate. Do you follow?"

"Um . . . ," I said.

"Ms. Martone, I do apologize for giving away your year-round-school article so abruptly to Ms. Bigley. Her accent played on my heartstrings, and I do know how it feels to be so far from home and without friends. I have walked in those shoes, and I hate to see someone else taking their first steps in them as I once did. That's why I did it. I do apologize and hope you will forgive me."

"Oh, Mr. Trigg, it wasn't my story anyway. And I do understand. It's fine now."

"Well, yes. I suppose it is. It certainly clarifies things for me. I understand from Mr. Lawrence that you've got a marvelous article for us for this issue anyway?"

I grinned. "I hope so!"

"Well, if it's anything like what he describes, I might have to assign you a regular fashion column!" He winked at me.

"Yeah, right!" I said. "Not for me, thanks. But I do have someone in mind who would be just perfect for the job. . . ."

"Great. We can discuss it after we put this issue to bed. Now, hurry out of here and pare down this overwrought column, please! You need to lighten up and lighten it up!"

I laughed. "Thanks, Mr. Trigg."

"No, thank you, Ms. Martone."

★　　★　　★

Well, the issue finally did come out, and you'll never guess what happened. My story—the school uniform story—was the front-page lead. And the year-round-school story wound up buried on page three! It was really well written but kind of boring. I thought about it, and it made sense: Michael was really good at the facts, but I was good at the quotes and about making it "relatable." I wasn't happy exactly, but just vindicated. It was good to know I wasn't so easily replaced and that I had been missed—by Michael and by Mr. Trigg.

Mr. Trigg comforted Michael by telling him it was a learning experience all around and that he was free to revisit the topic in a future issue, with or without a new cowriter.

My article got me lots of compliments. At lunch the day they published the online edition, tons of kids came up to me and congratulated me. I was sitting with Hailey, and she started to laugh after the third person came over.

"What?" I said.

"I'm starting to think maybe you *are* the best writer in the school."

"Oh, please. That was just pure egomania talking. I know better now."

"Well, I'm still the best soccer player, just so you know. And on my way to being the best watercolorist."

"Of that I have no doubt!" I laughed.

Just then Kate Bigley arrived. "Mind if I join you girls?" she asked.

"Not at all. Slide in!"

"Great article," said Kate, and Hailey and I burst out laughing.

"What?" said Kate, truly confused. "Was it something I said?"

"No, just don't fuel the egomaniac's fire," I said.

"Oh, Hailey, you're not an egomaniac," said Kate. "Now, Michael Lawrence, on the other hand . . ."

"Now Michael Lawrence what?" said Michael Lawrence himself, sliding his tray in next to mine.

"Hello, Mikey," I said.

"Great article," he said, and Kate, Hailey, and I cracked up. "Seriously. You're the star reporter," said Michael.

"Stop," I protested.

"Oh, that reminds me," said Hailey. She dove under the table and pulled something flat out of her bag and handed it to me. It was two sheets of cardboard taped together. "For you," she said with a flourish.

"Um, thanks?" I said.

"Open it!" she instructed. "Gently."

"Why are all my friends so bossy?" I said.

Hailey and Michael rolled their eyes at each other, but then Hailey turned back and watched me again eagerly.

I slit open the masking tape and peered inside. It was a piece of artwork of some kind. I slit another edge, and the two pieces of cardboard opened like a book. Inside was a beautiful watercolor signed by Hailey Jones with the date.

It was a picture of my beat-up, beloved messenger bag with my trusty notebook and a pencil propped next to it and a full-color edition of the *Cherry Valley Voice* with my byline on the article at the very top, above the fold (prime placement!). It was so realistic and beautiful and thoughtful that I started to cry.

"Whoa, girl! This is only like the third time I've seen you cry in all the years we've been friends!"

"It is so incredible, Hails. And so thoughtful and generous. I love it. I'll get it framed for my room."

Hailey grinned proudly.

"And I can definitely say you are the best artist in the school, hands down."

"Aw, go on!" said Hailey. There was a pause, and then Hailey said, "Really. Go on."

And we all laughed. I passed around Hailey's watercolor, cautioning everyone to be careful, and everyone oohed and ahhed over it. It was amazing, and I couldn't believe someone my age, let alone my very best friend, had done that painting.

"You are so lucky," said Kate, squeezing my shoulder.

"Lucky, nothing! It's hard work!" said Michael.

Just then Jeff Perry sat down at the table and started talking a mile a minute about how he'd just overheard Pfeiffer in the stairs ranting about how furious he is that the whole school wants uniforms now, how he never should have participated in my article, and how he always regrets it when he talks to the press!

I was thrilled. It's not that I like stirring up

trouble. I just like it when my work gets people talking. Then I sighed. Oh dear, I had just done an article with Mr. Pfeiffer where I'd thought it went well.

Michael looked at me, knowing what I was thinking.

"Don't worry, Pasty," he said. "Next time you interview him, I'll be there with you."

I grinned, and Kate squeezed my leg under the table and smiled.

I couldn't wait for the day to end so I could go home and show my mom Hailey's painting and discuss all the reactions to the new issue.

★   ★   ★

Finally I was at my locker, packing my messenger bag, and Michael walked up.

"Hey, so maybe we'll get assigned an article together for the next issue."

"That would be nice, for a change," I joked.

Michael didn't smile, though. "Listen, uh, Sam. Do you think . . . Would you ever want to go grab a slice of pizza or something? Even if, uh, we don't have an article together?"

"Oh, Mike! I thought you'd never ask!" I joked nervously.

He looked kind of hurt, so I had to be serious.

"Yes, Michael Lawrence. I would love to get pizza with you. Anytime. All the time. How's that?"

"Better," he said with a grin. "Hey, did you see the new Dear Know-It-All?"

Uh-oh. I'm totally convinced that he knows it's me who writes the column, and I'm always waiting for him to trip me up and somehow get me to confess it. I have to choose my words very carefully when he brings it up.

"Um, no. Why?" I said, the picture of innocence.

"It kind of reminded me of us. Did you write it?"

What????

"Um . . ."

"I mean, maybe I wrote it," he said with a half smile.

"*Did* you write it?" I asked, giddy with relief now that I knew he meant the question and not the answer.

"Maybe yes and maybe no."

"Well, what does it say?"

"I'm surprised you waited this long to ask me that. Are you sure you didn't write it?"

Oh dear.

"Just tell me!" I cried.

"It says, 'Dear Know-It-All. I miss my friend. We used to spend a lot of time together, but now we're both really busy and we don't see each other very often. I'm not sure what to say or do. Any advice? From, Feeling Left Out and Lonely.'" He looked at me.

"So did you write it?" I asked quietly. I was scared to breathe.

"No," he said, shaking his head. "But I could have. Did you?"

I gulped. "No." We were quiet for a minute. "But I could have," I said.

He nodded.

"So what did he say?"

"Who?" Michael asked.

"Dear Know-It-All?"

"Oh. She said, 'Dear Lonely: Don't despair. Just tell your friend you miss him or her. It's really that simple. Good luck, KIA.'"

"I noticed you called Know-It-All a 'she,'" I said bravely.

"And I noticed you called Know-It-All a 'he,'" said Michael.

I shrugged. "Maybe it's you."

"I couldn't fill those shoes," he said.

"How do you know?" I asked.

"They're girls' shoes." He smiled and shrugged, starting to walk away.

"Hey, Mikey?"

"Yeah?" he said without turning around.

"I miss you!"

"I miss you, too, Pasty." *Journalist Struck by Cupid's Arrow Dies of Love in Hall.*

Oh boy. I couldn't wait for the next issue. Or the next meeting tomorrow, when I'd sit next to Michael Lawrence and we'd get assigned another article. I made a mental note to ask Allie for some outfit advice. All I could think about was what shoes I'd wear.

Extra! Extra!

Want the scoop on what Samantha is up to next?

Here's a sneak peek of the eighth book in the Dear Know-It-All series:

Texting 1, 2, 3

BREAKING NEWS: YOUNG GIRL MELTS ON SIDEWALK DURING RECORD HEAT

It's hot. Right now as I sit on my front steps waiting for my BFF, Hailey Jones, and her mom to take us to the air-conditioned mall on the third day of an awful heat wave, it's the kind of hot that makes me wonder if I could actually dissolve into a unrecognizable blob of goo by the time Hailey gets here. Breaking News: *Young Girl Melts on Sidewalk During Record Heat* is what I'm thinking.

It's also the kind of hot that makes me wish for a chill in the air and sweaters and, believe it or not, school. School just goes with fall. School also goes with seeing my forever and ever crush, Michael Lawrence, every day. I haven't seen him since the town's Fourth of July fireworks display, which was awesome. Hailey, Michael and his friend Frank, and I all went together. I couldn't really call it a double date since Hailey says she doesn't have a crush on Frank, but he definitely has a crush on her and maybe one of these days Hailey will like him back. Hailey says he's a really nice guy, but his hair is too dark and his ears are too big for her taste. I think she's actually afraid to like someone she knows has a big crush on her. But that secret's just between me and me.

The only thing that bums me out about the start of school is that I've finished my tenure as Dear Know-It-All, the anonymous (I think!) advice columnist. It was a year-long gig, and since I did it all last year, my time is up. I can't imagine not doing it, but I guess I'll have more time to focus on the other writing I do for the paper.

I've been obsessing about who the new Know-It-All will be all summer, but I guess I'll never know since it's top secret. I managed never to blow my cover, as far as I know. That wasn't an easy job, but I really grew to love it and found that every time I had to give advice to someone else, I learned something new about myself. Still, it was a lot of stress. Maybe it will be good to focus on other things now. Like not melting.

Finally just in the nick of time, Hailey's white car pulled up. The sun glared on it so brightly, I had to shield my eyes just to look at it. I was sweating after walking the twenty feet to the car.

"Ugh, I'm surprised I didn't melt!" I said, slumping down into the backseat. The A/C was blasting in the car. "It feels so good in here."

"I know," Hailey said from the front. "You have A/C in your house, though, don't you?"

"Yeah, but my mom is always turning it off when we're not in the house."

"Us too," Hailey's mom said. "It always costs a fortune!"

"Well, at least walking around the ice-cold mall is free," Hailey said. "Unless you buy stuff."

"And speaking of buying stuff, my mom gave me some money for a back-to-school outfit," I said, holding up my shoulder bag as if Hailey could see the money inside.

"I did the same for Hailey," Mrs. Jones said. "I used to love getting together the perfect back-to-school outfit. It would take me weeks," she added dreamily.

"Yeah, well, I just want to be cool and comfortable," Hailey said, rolling her eyes, ever practical. She wasn't one to fuss over her clothes unless a boy was involved.

I just nodded, but secretly I wanted to get the cutest outfit I could possibly find for Michael. Since he hadn't seen me in a while, it was a chance to wow him a little bit. It's not that I wanted to look different, just a little new, I guess. I should have asked my older sister, Allie, for some advice. She always looks great.

"I don't know," Hailey said as I tried on a red tank top with ruffles down the front. "It's not really you."

"Yeah, but what if I wanted to try out a new look?" I said, looking past her in the mirror and flipping my hair from side to side. I knew it was a little much, but I felt like taking a risk.

"I think what you're looking for is the

You-Only-Better top, not the Who-Are-You? top, which is what *that* is," she said, pointing at me. Then she held up a blousy white cotton shirt.

"Nah, kind of boring," I said, waving the white shirt away. I already had a few blouses like it.

"What about this one?" Hailey said, and held up a purple tunic style tee with a really cool green design embroidered on the front.

"Hmmm," I said. "It would look nice with those leggings." I pointed to a simple black pair. I grabbed it from Hailey and tried it on. It was supercute, and the green embroidery highlighted my eyes.

"Perfect! You only better," Hailey said.

"Why not just me? Why the better part?" I asked.

"I'm just kidding with you, beauty queen," Hailey said, grinning. She went and tried on a white T-shirt, the kind that she had a million of.

I looked around quickly and grabbed a plain turquoise tank top. The color would look fantastic on her, and it wasn't frilly or anything.

"Okay, okay," she said, and disappeared into

the dressing room with the tank top. She came out looking amazing. That was the thing with Hailey. It didn't take much for her to look great.

"See, it makes you look even tanner! And those white capris look perfect with it."

Hailey was looking in the mirror, a big smile spreading across her face.

"Okay, you win," she said.

When I came home, the house felt nice and cool since my mother and Allie were home and the A/C had been blasting for a while. I went into the kitchen and got a peach and sat at the counter. One of my favorite things about summer was peaches. I ate at least one a day. I took a big bite, and the juice dribbled down my chin.

My mom came into the kitchen and handed me a napkin.

"Thanks," I said, and wiped my mouth.

"Did you see my note that Mr. Trigg called?" Mom said.

I looked at the phone. There was a pink sticky note on it. I squinted my eyes. *Sam! Mr. Trigg called. Call him back. 555-1873.*

"Sam?" my mom said in a worried tone. "Are you okay?"

"Uh, yeah," I said, snapping back into reality. "I should call him back." I got up, threw my peach pit away, and took the phone into the den. I paused for a moment before dialing. Then I took a deep breath and went for it.

"Hello?" said Mr. Trigg's peppy British-accented voice. I had to admit I'd missed it.

"Hi, Mr. Trigg. This is Sam . . ." I paused. "Martone?" I said a little unsteadily.

"Ms. Martone! How has your summer been? Brilliant, I hope?" he chirped at me.

"Yes, um, brilliant," I said back cautiously.

"Well, I have a little business to discuss with you," he said. I could tell there was an edge of excitement in his voice, but then again, there was always an edge of excitement in his voice.

"I would like you to have another go at the column," he said.

Did he mean what I think he meant? "The Dear Know-It-All column?" I asked tentatively.

"No, the lunch menu column. Of course I'm

asking about the Know-It-All column!"

"Oh," I said, my head spinning with confusion.

"You don't sound happy." Mr. Trigg sounded a bit disappointed.

"No, I'm . . ." I paused. I couldn't believe it, actually. "I'm thrilled! And surprised. Isn't it just a one-year thing?" I asked.

"Ms. Martone, the great thing about being the newspaper advisor is that I get to make the rules. You got the best responses last year that any Know-It-All has ever had. The position is yours again, if you'll have it."

My face flushed. "Wow, I don't know what to say."

"Say you'll do it!" Mr. Trigg cleared his throat. "I mean, if you feel you're up for it. Same deal as last year—top secret. And if for some reason you say yes now and change your mind, I need to know in the next day or two."

It did mean the stress again and adding more to my workload, but it was one of the coolest things I've done in my short career as a writer. How could I not do it? I just hoped I could keep it a secret from Hailey, Michael, and Allie for one more year.

"Of course I'll do it!" I declared.

"Excellent!" Mr. Trigg said. "We have a staff meeting on the first day of school. Three p.m. sharp. I'll see you then."

I said good-bye and hung up. My face still felt warm. It was a really nice ego boost to be asked again. I had to tell someone the good news. I was bursting! Luckily, my mom was allowed to know my secret . . . again.

"Mom," I called. She didn't answer, and I didn't want Allie to wonder why I was yelling. I found her in the kitchen where I'd left her. She was standing up eating a peach and reading the paper. I glanced around to make sure Allie wasn't anywhere.

"I'm doing it again," I whispered in a low conspiratorial voice.

My mom lowered the paper and put down her peach down on a napkin in front of her. "Doing what?" she whispered back.

"I'm going to be Dear Know-It-All again. Mr. Trigg said I got the best responses from any other Know-It-All and he wants me to do another year." This time I wasn't so quiet.

"That's great!" Mom said. "You must be proud of yourself."

I nodded, beaming. Then I heard another voice in the kitchen.

"Why should she be proud of herself?" Allie called from the hallway.

"Because . . . ," Mom said, and looked at me helplessly.

"Because Mr. Trigg called and said he wants me to do even more stories for the paper this year!" I blurted out. I saw my mom let out a breath.

Allie came padding barefoot in the kitchen. She had her hair up in a towel and a green facial mask covering her face. "Oh, big deal," she said, and then turned on her heel and walked out. Phew.

One more year of being Dear Know-It-All—I hoped I could do it!